ORBITAL ECLIPSE

THE SECOND LUNAR LOVESCAPE NOVEL

ESSIE POWERS

BESPOKE ALIMENTATION PROTOCOL

*A*licia *Brennan* reached up and brushed the chopped, brunette fringe free of her eyes. Some days she wondered if she might ever suck up the courage to simply get all her hair buzz cut clean off . . . but other days—other *nights*—she was glad that she'd left herself enough to toy with.

Left enough for *others* to toy with . . .

As she levered the oven door open wide, she felt the burst of heat leak out from within.

It brought the colour out in her cheeks.

She recalled how an *ex*-boyfriend had once commented on her complexion while cooking, saying that she looked like an overripe beetroot. Although she had laughed it off at the time, the comment had continued to sting many years later. Cooking had always been her passion, and she'd often find herself checking her appearance in whatever mirror she might be able to locate nearby; worrying about whether he might've been telling the truth.

It had even put her off cooking for *future* boyfriends.

She had been young and naïve when that *particular* boyfriend had made the comment. These days she would never—*ever*—allow a comment like that to slide.

Could that be the reason why she was all alone?

Was that the reason why she'd closed herself away from the majority of humankind on the Moon? Because she was cold . . . because she was wary of allowing *anybody* close?

Turning her attention away from DIY-psychoanalysis, she took in the contents of the oven. She was far from pleased with the state of the Mooncakes within. True, they weren't burned. And neither were they crude.

But something—*something*—just wasn't right.

She slipped on the oven gloves she'd brought up here from Earth. The gloves had a collection of stars and crescent Moons spotted across them in a haphazard design. They had been her parents' idea of a joke when she had taken up the contract with Celestial Stays—when she had decided to dedicate a significant portion of her life, or at the very least her *youth*, to the Moon.

The gloves themselves had received several burns, of course. But rather than toss them out and replace them with a pair of standard-issue ones—as was no doubt required by some lunar health and safety regulation or other—she had held onto them out of sentimental value.

"All righty," she said to herself, reaching into the oven, tightening her grip about the baking tray. "All righty, all righty, all righty."

It happened quickly. So quickly that she hardly had time to process the sensation in her brain before she acted.

The intense heat through her gloves.

Melting through her buttery skin.

She acted before thinking, releasing her hold on the tray;

allowing it to drop. It fell to the floor with a clatter. The Mooncakes scattered to all parts. Their delicate pastry crumbling and flaking.

Forever ruined.

"*Shit!*" she cried out, loudly . . . loud enough so that the customers in the Orbital Café—*if there had been any customers*— would've heard her loud and clear.

She slipped her hands free of the oven gloves and sucked on the afflicted fingers—the ones which'd received the worst of the burns.

If one of her members of staff had made a similar fuss over such a simple matter as a burned hand, she would've been quick to reprimand them. All the same, swearing at the top of one's voice was hardly becoming for a Guardian—for a senior member of the Celestial Stays team.

Thankfully there was nobody around to reprimand *her*.

The only person who could conceivably reprimand her at all was the Supervisor of Catering—her *boss*—Habiba Nuha. And, mercifully, she hadn't shown her face.

Not *yet*, in any case.

Alicia froze in place, still unable to quite square what she'd done.

She took stock of the scene.

Mooncakes all over the floor.

Fluffy scraps of pastry scattered all about.

It took just about everything within her not to swear again.

She had spent almost the entire morning putting together the Mooncakes. She had taken almost painstaking care with each one, attempting to get them completely, one-hundred-per-cent right. So that they might hold up to the elite reputation of Celestial Stays.

And now she'd gone and tossed all that work across the floor.

She glanced over her oven gloves another time, seeing that there was now a collection of sizeable holes in the fabric. No wonder she had managed to burn herself. In her frustration, she unceremoniously tossed them across the room where they nestled neatly into the bin.

She was so furious—so wound up—that she didn't even take so much as a moment to admire her achievement.

How many times had she tossed this, that or the other in the direction of the bin, only for tossed item to fall short, or else smack into the wall?

She went off to go fetch a dustpan and brush. It wouldn't be right for her to palm off her own mess on some unsuspecting droid or drone.

This was her responsibility.

That was one thing her parents had taught her back home on the family farm, in Wood Dale, Illinois. Honesty in owning up to her mistakes.

It took quarter of an hour to clean up the mess to her satisfaction.

Once she'd returned the dustpan and brush to their designated cupboards, she inspected herself in a nearby, full-length mirror, smoothing out the collar of her royal-blue, Celestial Stays overalls.

She brushed a few rogue flecks of pastry from the silver Guardian's patch sewn onto her breast pocket. It seemed that the whole episode had flustered her somewhat. She didn't like mess, and she *hated* making mistakes. And it was all the stranger because she almost *never* made mistakes of any kind.

Just what had she been thinking?

Her attention to detail had brought her far in the Celestial Stays organisation. And she had assumed that it would raise her higher still.

From the frank discussions Alicia had shared with her boss, Habiba Nuha, she had deduced that Habiba was thinking seriously about taking retirement. About turning down her next rotation on Luna. And there was only one name which would surely pop up— which would be the *obvious* choice for the next Supervisor of Catering.

Or, at least, *Alicia* saw it that way.

Already, she had made up her mind. If she wasn't made Supervisor of Catering when Habiba surely announced her resignation then she would resign. She had always nurtured the idea of starting up her own little bakery down on Earth. Nothing fancy— nothing like *that*. But it seemed a crime to allow her grandmother's recipes to go to waste.

Especially since she had been the first in her family to try them out on the Moon.

"I thought you'd be done by now."

Alicia turned to look.

Saw who stood in the doorway.

Julius Denisov.

She took in his smirking expression. Her gaze seemed almost to bounce off his heavily gelled black hair, which coincidentally made him look more like some sort of an action figure than an actual living, breathing human being.

Maybe if Alicia could find some proof that he wasn't in fact a human being then she might be able to justify his murder. But there she went again, with misanthropic thoughts . . .

It sickened her to think that she had ever seen *anything* in Julius.

And what sickened her more was that she had had to see for herself.

Lunar romances. Yeah, no matter how good of an idea they

seemed in the heat of the moment, they were certainly something she wouldn't be doing again any time soon . . .

Although, like all other employees, Julius wore the navy-blue overalls of Celestial Stays, Alicia was certain that he would've looked far more at home in a tuxedo; a white handkerchief protruding from the breast pocket. Back home, in St Petersburg, he had once told her that he had worked at a casino. Just like he worked at the lunar casino now—the Stellar Tide.

As he lurked in the doorway, he rubbed his index finger and thumb together, as if he was unconsciously looking for some kind of bribe. "I told the Wei clan that the Mooncakes would be with them in time for the Mid-Autumn Festival."

The Wei family had arrived to the Celestial Stays Dome a couple of nights ago. As was in keeping with the exclusive, bespoke service offered to lunar guests, the Hospitality Division left no stone unturned when researching customers' habits; wanting to make them feel right at home, even here, on the Moon.

Alicia allowed this to sink in.

"The celebrations don't begin until tomorrow night," she said.

Here Julius gave a wry grin.

Alicia had to restrain herself from punching his lights out right there and then.

Why didn't he just keep to himself?

Why did he seem so determined to make her life a misery at each and every opportunity available?

He took a couple of steps into the kitchen.

And Alicia almost made for his throat.

If there was one way to truly turn her from the doe-eyed, baby deer she often imagined herself, then it was by encroaching on the one place she felt truly comfortable. Her kitchen.

Casually, Julius crouched down. Only when he rose back up did

Alicia see what it was that he held. A piece of Mooncake. A piece which had managed to escape her cleaning efforts. She stared at the fragment of Mooncake which Julius held: a personal affront to her cleaning efforts.

He brought the piece of Mooncake up to his mouth.

Parted his lips.

Unable to help herself, Alicia trod forward.

"Don't," she said, reaching out for the piece of Mooncake.

Julius brought the Mooncake down from his lips momentarily. He slipped her another wry-mouthed smirk, and then, with such a slick wink that she might easily have not seen it at all, he popped it into his mouth.

It was then that Alicia lost it.

She grappled for his throat.

Seized hold of him.

Staring him in his surprised eyes, she said, "Spit it out! Spit it out *now!*"

Julius's complexion quickly shifted.

His pallid skin tone became quite red.

His shoulders hunched.

And he began to cough.

Choking.

When Alicia released him, Julius swiftly turned his back to her and spat out the offending piece of Mooncake. He bent over himself, hands on his kneecaps, as he regained his posture.

Alicia allowed herself a wry smile of her own, savouring the moment.

Finally, apparently having got his breath back again, Julius turned to face her; his eyes wide, his colour still a little blushed from the exertion. "You *bitch!*" he said. "What the *hell* was that all about?" He shook his head, screwing up his eyes as he headed for the kitchen doorway. "I just wanted a little taste."

He shook his head even more as he trod out into the corridor, and away from Alicia's kitchen. She was fairly certain she heard him utter, "*Mad* bitch," under his breath, but she wouldn't have been able to swear it.

As she turned her attention to cleaning up the piece of Mooncake which Julius had spit out on the floor, she thought with no small amount of pride about how Julius had been one of those men who'd tried to control her—who had tried to *put her in her place . . .* well, he'd simply ended up where all the others had done.

On the scrapheap.

2

DESIGNATED RECREATIONAL
PERIOD

licia had nearly forgotten all about Julius by the time she got back to the Basements; the area of the Celestial Stays Dome dedicated to employees. Thinking long and hard about treating herself to a few laps in the swimming pool—to drying herself out in the sauna—she jabbed a finger into her inner-ear, checking in with the neural transmitter placed in her frontal lobe, which, in turn, checked in with the Link.

The Link informed her that the pool was packed out.

The sauna too.

With a sigh, she returned to her apartment, realising that she would have to console herself with a hot shower.

Towel wrapped about her midriff, she trudged about her apartment. She paused to inspect the various dressmaking dummies she had set up throughout; to look over the clothing designs she was working on. The guests themselves had their own tailors department located within the Lunar Grand, but those tailors weren't allowed to extend their services to employees.

So that was where Alicia came in.

Although Alicia had never given it so much as a second thought at the time, she supposed that in all her years of vagabonding she had acquired an unusual set of skills.

There was her passion for baking, of course, but that had come from her grandmother; that had come to her through her upbringing on the family farm.

But the other skills, as well as the more *exotic* recipes, had come about because she'd decided to leave the cosy little farm—with its apple blossoms and beehives—behind.

Alicia could still recall learning how to make Mooncakes from a matriarch up in the Tian Shan mountains of China. She could still recall the inquisitive expressions on the faces of the people who inhabited the remote villages she'd passed through on her travels; and how they'd asked her so many questions. And she had done her very best to respond to them in her faltering Mandarin.

Indeed, it'd been with the full Moon shining down on the village that the old lady had set about mixing up the ingredients in the stone bowl she apparently used for all of her baking. And Alicia had watched on—and breathed *deep*—as the Mooncakes had been set to cook within the clay oven. As for the dressmaking, well, that had come about while Alicia had been in South Africa.

Finding herself somewhat short of funds, she had managed to hustle herself up a job in a local clothing factory. Although the work had been tough—and she'd felt somewhat out of place as the rest of the factory workers spoke among themselves in their own languages—she had learned valuable lessons about all aspects of tailoring.

And she put them all into practice with all the most modern methods.

Why, she recalled the dress she had designed for Louise—her

friend who worked in the Crescent Gardens. She had taken a simple, classic design and then used virtual fabrics to create an unbeatable, fully customisable colour scheme.

Afterwards, Alicia could recall how Karolin Köhler herself—owner of Celestial Stays—had been rumoured to ask after the origin of Louise's dress. And, of course, as was the state of gossip about the Celestial Stays Dome, Frau Köhler had come to Alicia personally asking after her design work; asking her if she didn't see herself ever working in the Lunar Grand with the other tailors in Hospitality. And Alicia had had to simply inform her that it wasn't her passion; and she had to remind her that the Schwarzwälder Kirschtorte—the *Black Forest Gâteau*—she had tried at the Orbital Café, and complimented so roundly, had also been her responsibility. It was only then that Alicia saw that Frau Köhler truly understood.

And Alicia had remained where she was.

With her passion.

Cooking.

Alicia settled into an armchair. She stared at her reflection in her wallpaper; currently set to its mirror mode. She couldn't help but note the dark circles which clung to the bottoms of her eyes. Somehow those dark circles reminded her of the colour of those soggy-bottomed clouds which'd linger on the horizon of the family farm. And it brought back with it the smell of *rain* in the air. The way that the moisture almost reached right out and *stroked* her cheeks.

The stillness before a storm.

She breathed in deeply, taking the air right down to the pit of her stomach.

And then she sighed it right back out again.

Maybe . . . maybe she *was* ready to go home.

Perhaps she was ready to return to Earth.

This whole *Moon* thing had certainly been a great experience; something which was wonderful to have tucked beneath her belt; and yet she couldn't help wondering at all the places in the world she hadn't yet seen . . . all those *people* she hadn't yet *met*.

Hadn't she spent long enough up here, in space, slaving over a hot stove; losing herself in the gorgeous, intoxicating odours of her past?

Her earpiece gave her a short, sharp vibration.

Bringing her back to the present.

She blinked a couple of times.

Ridding herself of the daze she'd fallen into.

Finally, she focussed on the message the Link fed her.

About the party tonight.

She had had so much on her mind—what with those Moon-cakes that needed to be prepared for the following day; and with Julius unceremoniously barging in on her—that she'd clean forgotten about it.

When she saw what the locale was to be, she almost dismissed the message out of hand; almost notified the Link to leave her be until it was time for tomorrow's shift.

The Stellar Tide Casino.

Julius.

Eugh.

It didn't bear thinking about.

And yet, here she was, sitting on her chair—in her apartment; all alone—*thinking* about it . . . and, much to her disgust, she was thinking about *him*.

With another deep breath, and another great sigh, she rose up off the armchair. She couldn't help thinking about a piece of advice her grandmother had given her when she'd been much younger; around the time that boyfriend had remarked on her penchant for going all red while she was cooking. Her grandmother had told her—in no uncertain terms—that there were Good Apples, and there were Bad Apples. And nothing in-between.

'Oh,' she had told Alicia, long ago, 'don't get me wrong—it's all a matter of perception. Why, somebody's Good Apple, might just as well be another one's Bad Apple. That's the thing with humans, see? We're not objective. We're opinionated, fallible.' And then she'd shake her head as if the silliness of it all had tickled her just right, and add, 'Ain't that just the truth?'

Each and every time, Alicia would just smile and nod along, never really understanding . . . until, one day, she did.

And now, without a doubt, she understood clear and clean *just* what her grandmother had been telling her.

Sure, for her—*for Alicia Brennan*—Julius Denisov was a Bad Apple, but that didn't mean for somebody else he might not be a Good Apple.

The trick, Alicia saw now, was to know how to pick the Good Apples from the bad.

But that was easier said than done.

All the same, she wasn't about to allow some *Bad Apple* to dictate the terms by which she would live her life. She *would* go to the ball, *Goddammit!*

In the end, Alicia settled for one of the dresses she had designed for Louise; the one with the dynamic fabrics. She eventually decided on an elegant blue-and-green tartan design; one of those which she recalled from the month she'd spent in Edinburgh,

Scotland . . . she recalled how she'd had a beau for a while there: a Jock, or Alec, or something . . . had he played bagpipes, or was it just her imagination?

Because she couldn't face turning up at the Stellar Tide alone, Alicia went to stop in on Louise before doing anything further. In addition to using the Link to inform Louise that she was at the door, Alicia was certain to actually *physically* knock too.

She could never be too careful with Louise.

Not now that she and Njhay were impossible to part.

Alicia had always found it difficult to imagine herself with only one man; to somehow *throw* herself so quickly and dizzy-headedly at a single man. What if in her case there were many—*many*—Good Apples to be found?

And it wasn't like her to miss out . . .

Although Njhay was present in Louise's apartment, the two of them were a respectful few paces apart. They were wearing their party clothes; Louise in a neat, prim, emerald-green corset over the top of a creamy peach skirt, while Njhay was in his tuxedo . . . just as she imagined Julius would turn himself out that evening.

Once again, Alicia cursed to herself, almost as if she might be able to force Julius—and all memory of him—from her mind by pure will alone. Perhaps it was because he had been her first and, thus far, *only* romance on the Moon. That must be it.

"Well," Louise said, craning her pretty, blond head in Alicia's direction; her British accent strong even though she'd only spoken a single syllable. "You're not looking your usual self."

Alicia gave her a slight smile by way of reply.

She liked how she had the power to take people off-guard.

She secretly *loved* the alchemy which'd gone into her upbringing. The one which'd given her an innocent, lash-batting, Illinois farm girl's exterior with an infernal longing for passion and new experiences barely held concealed within.

And it played into her hands all the time.

"Oh," Alicia replied, answering Louise's question, "I made a bit of a mess in the kitchen."

"Nothing cleaning droids can't fix," Njhay put in from where he sat on the edge of the bed, lacing up his dress shoes.

As a scientist, working in the laboratory based in the Crescent Gardens, Alicia well knew that Njhay was speaking from experience. She knew that scientists could quite easily make just as much of a mess as chefs. But she also knew that they took *far* less pride in the cleanliness of their workspace; that, indeed, if it hadn't been for the cleaning droids then their labs might just as likely have resembled the proverbial pigsties of her childhood.

When Louise finally caught Alicia's eye, she felt the zip pass between them. That little bolt of lightning which Alicia could only ever think to describe by the wishy-washy term 'intuition'. From that moment on, it only took a single glance from Louise to Njhay to send him scarpering from the room, mumbling something about having brought the wrong bowtie.

Once the two women were alone, Louise sat down on the bed beside Alicia. She laid her hand down on her thigh and peered into her eyes. Alicia felt a warm stirring in her gut. It was funny, she had always thought of herself as being a resilient individual—she'd always believed herself to be *independent*. She'd grown up an only child and had always been able to make her own fun, or 'be her own friend', as her parents were always imploring her. And she'd always believed that the cows, the pigs, the horses, the meadows, the sweeping lake, and the harvest Moons were all her friends . . . but there was something which they couldn't give her.

Empathy.

After all, it was only nature.

Only *animals*.

The strangest thing which struck her was that Louise sitting here, beside her, was really the first person she would ever consider to be her friend . . . someone she had allowed close to her who *wasn't* a lover of some kind.

"What did he do *this* time?" Louise said, her tone of voice firm, no-nonsense.

Alicia recalled her first impressions of Louise, when the two of them had met here—in her apartment. Alicia had been called into action to help suit Louise out for an evening function. She had brought her the dress which Alicia herself was wearing tonight.

She had believed Louise to be skittish, to be a touch twitchy. She had thought that she was just another in a long line of naïve girls who thought it might be 'fun' to go and work on the Moon. But soon enough Alicia had realised that she and Louise weren't really all that different. The two of them shared a common secret. They possessed an inner steel which they held deep within themselves; a place where, most of the time, it would remain *hidden*.

But during that unfortunate episode with Alex Barn—Louise's former lover—Louise had put her inner steel on show for all to see for themselves.

And Alicia, for one, would never forget.

Alicia turned her mind back to the question; to how she had referenced Julius.

It pained her that she had to keep coming back to him.

That she seemed *unable* to put him out of her life once and for all.

"In the café," Alicia began, "I was preparing the Mooncakes, doing some *trial* recipes, and he . . . well, you know . . ."

"Showed up without permission?"

Alicia gave a firm nod, knowing how *stupid* she sounded.

How *oversensitive*.

And yet, Louise understood instinctively just how important the kitchen at the Orbital Café was for her. That it was much more than a simple kitchen; that it was a *refuge*.

Julius had violated that.

Louise squeezed her thigh.

Alicia smirked. "He picked up one of the Mooncakes I dropped on the floor—I'm pretty sure he nearly choked to death on it as a consequence."

Louise smiled wider. "Well, I don't imagine he'll be back in a hurry, in that case."

"I'd be so lucky," Alicia replied.

Because it felt like she should, Alicia let out a laugh. But even to herself it sounded hollow—*forced*.

"Come on," Louise said, taking hold of the crook of Alicia's arm, "I'm sure that the party'll cheer you up. There's nothing like the Banquet Hall to chase away the blues."

As Alicia felt herself being lifted to her feet, being escorted to the door, she couldn't help wondering if she wasn't making some big mistake.

If the best thing she couldn't do right now was to take that dip in the pool—indulge herself in that angelic-sounding sauna—and then get an early night.

But, despite all the hard-headedness she'd developed in her years of travelling, none of it seemed sufficient for her to tell Louise no; that she wouldn't be attending the party that evening.

So she had no choice but to go.

3

CONCILIATORY PROCEDURE

*I*f *Alicia* hadn't been certain that going to the party at the Stellar Tide had been a big mistake, she was by the time she heard the rampant bassline throbbing through the floor. The mystical magic of the music somehow grappled her by the bones, drawing her closer, while, in equal measure, pushing her further and further away.

As she stood on Njhay and Louise's heels—the two of them walking arm in arm ahead of her—she knew that she was positioned on the precipice; that she could either keep on going or she could cut her losses and turn right back around.

Through the doorway to the Banquet Hall, she could make out the swirling, multi-coloured lights. She could already hear the *thrum* of conversation. And, she was certain, the body heat emanating from within . . .

As Alicia had found out about herself long ago, she didn't do too well without skin-on-skin contact over long periods.

Like this period.

She made a promise to herself—to stick close to Njhay and Louise. She would be the mythical third wheel that she had so many times made fun of . . . but, at the very least, if she *did* feel the urge for that old skin-on-skin feeling then she could get it from Louise.

When they left the hallway, sedately lit with flame-orange bulbs, behind, Alicia immediately found herself blindsided by the constant flurry of noise and bright lights. She squeezed her eyes tight as if it might help her to make better sense of her new surroundings, but it only succeeded in making them all the more opaque.

As she tailed Njhay and Louise through the crowds of clustered-up bodies, she could already feel herself slipping into introversion. It had been one of her defence mechanisms while she'd been on the road. Whenever she felt overwhelmed by a culture, by a new experience, she would delve deep into her thoughts. She supposed she drew on the skill of imagination which she'd developed back when she'd spent endless hours alone on the family farm. Whenever she returned to that place it was like a safe house for her; something in her imagination which would always remain.

She recognised familiar faces among the attendees.

All of them fellow employees, of course.

There were strict rules about the Celestial Stays hired help mingling with guests.

This was an *employee-only* party.

Among the faces, Alicia noted William Duval—the Security Division Supervisor. As always, he looked stern. Tonight, though, his throbbing biceps were kept under wraps by his tuxedo, and his white hair seemed to lend him an almost grandfatherly air.

Not that Alicia would've said so much out loud to his face.

His wife hung off his elbow, and Alicia couldn't help but note the sour expression which seemed to linger across her features. While partners were allowed to make the trip with Supervisor- and Guardian-level employees, it was an infrequent sight. Whether it was because the role was unpaid, or because those attracted to working under the Celestial Stays Dome tended to be *solitary* types, Alicia wasn't too sure.

One thing was for certain, with no duties to see to—nothing to do except wait for the husband or wife to return from their day's work—Alicia imagined all sorts of fancies fleeted through the unoccupied partner's mind . . . inevitably those which featured younger, more attractive members of the opposite sex. Of which, at least in Supervisor Duval's case, Alicia realised she was one.

Another Alicia recognised among the crowd was Supervisor Mbemba, who ran the Tourism Division; responsible for every- thing from tours out to the Lunar One crash site, and the surrounding areas, to guided excursions to the Lunar Caverns. It was impossible to hear anything Supervisor Mbemba said for the music.

Finally, Alicia made it through to the other side of the dance floor.

When she cast a glance back over the clustered-up dancers, she realised that she had unintentionally jettisoned Louise and Njhay.

Now, though, looking at them, seeing the two of them with smiles threatening to bust free of their lips as they twirled about in one another's arms, Alicia couldn't bring herself to weigh them down.

Instead, she headed for the large, glass double doors of the Banquet Hall which offered a view of the Celestial Stays Dome. They had been thrown open specifically for the party.

It felt good to have the cool sensation of the ventilation systems blowing back against her cheeks.

She looked out over the landscape, first taking in the half-buried building of the Basements; the place she called home. She felt a dull thrill through her stomach to take in the sight, surely some part of her *demanding* that she turn around right away and tuck herself into bed. As always, she had some serious work tomorrow at the café, what with that Mooncake recipe to perfect. She should've been channelling her thought power through her hands, and into her cooking.

But now she'd only succeeded in making herself feel depressed.

Once her gaze moved beyond the Basements, it was of course impossible not to take in the cylindrical building of the Lunar Grand which grew up out of the dunes. There was a constant buzz of PEARs—Personal Transporters—passing through the entrance marquee. All of the rich and famous. Unlike other members of staff who she could name, Alicia felt no resentment at all for the wealthy guests. In fact, it was truer to say that she *empathised* with them. If she'd been in the same position—*rich*—she would no doubt have made the journey up to the Moon.

Those who travelled up here were after her own heart, she decided.

Sure, they might have more money than they could conceivably spend in many lifetimes, but they had adventurous spirits after her own.

Just peeping out from behind the Lunar Grand, Alicia took in the Armstrong Archive; its wave-like design sitting on the very fringes of the Celestial Stays Dome. In a way, she supposed that it was a kind of visual representation of Celestial Stays's mission statement.

As per the terms of their lease on the Moon, they were required to provide space for academic research . . . and this was realised through the Armstrong Archive and the laboratories at the Crescent Gardens—the labs where Njhay worked.

As Alicia reached out and grasped hold of the chilled balcony railing, she couldn't help but notice the Crescent Gardens themselves, as they swept through the whole of the Dome, providing a much-needed verdant touch; differentiation from the unending grey-white, lunar dust.

Further away, she took in Entry Clearance; the Lunar Rover and Shuttle Pool, all of those procedures which she, and any new member of staff—or guest, for that matter—had to pass through before setting foot here, beneath the dome.

Finally, her gaze brought her back to what she could truthfully call the only part of the Moon which was vaguely, in some way, hers.

The Orbital Café.

She recalled how when she'd first arrived to the Moon—when she'd first laid eyes on the Orbital Café, with its faux-Alpine chalet appearance . . . those 'Christmas' red and greens, as Louise had once described them to her—she had believed it to be somewhat kitsch.

In fact, she had almost put her foot in it just a week into her employment by confiding her opinions in her boss, Supervisor Habiba.

Habiba had briskly informed Alicia that the whole design had been Frau Karolin Köhler's idea; something of a nostalgic throwback to one of her childhood memories.

After all this time, Alicia had to admit that the Orbital Café's appearance had grown on her to such a degree that she couldn't imagine it looking any different.

Because if she was frank with herself—and if Frau Karolin Köhler was frank with *herself*—then there wasn't exactly a lot that *wasn't* kitsch about humans setting up a luxury resort on the surface of the Moon.

Just then, as Alicia found her eyes inevitably drifting to the periphery of the Dome, and taking in the green-blue orb of Earth which hovered up in the sky above, she heard a voice from behind her.

"Alicia? Could I have a word?"

When Alicia turned, she found herself nose-to-nose with Mbemba, Supervisor of the Tourism Division.

Alicia pushed away all of the thoughts which littered her mind.

And she put on a smile.

She needed to turn on the Illinois farm-girl charm if she truly intended to get on within the Celestial Stays structure.

Before Alicia really had the chance to catch her breath, she found Supervisor Mbemba whisking her away. Away from the balcony where Alicia had been taking in the Dome spread out before her, and back—*briefly*—through the Banquet Hall, with its raucous music, and grinding, dancing bodies. Supervisor Mbemba finally brought Alicia to a smaller room which sat alongside the Banquet Hall.

A room where the music wasn't so obtrusive.

It was a space lit with candles, leaving it in a sober, twilight. She could make out dark forms within the smaller room. All of them standing up—each of them cradling a drink at their chest.

Although the consumption of alcohol was strictly prohibited on the Moon, it was one of those rules which seemed easily bent at will by both staff and guests alike.

From the tone of laughter bellowing forth from some of the

people collected here, Alicia was left in no doubt that a good proportion of the room was inebriated.

She had stopped drinking a long time ago—back when she'd been twenty-one, or twenty-two.

She had made the decision when she'd overindulged in some rice liquor at this Japanese bar in the middle of nowhere.

It'd been shocking to wake up in an unfamiliar bed, being tended to by a concerned elderly couple who—as she'd learned through a combination of gestures and single-word Basic phrases —had come across her lying in a gutter, out for the count.

Somehow without any harm having come to her . . .

It'd been almost like a horse's hoof to the centre of the fore-head; ramming home just truly how alone she was on her travels. That, with no one nearby who loved her—who was *looking out for her*—she would need to look out for herself.

And that started with keeping her wits about her.

Apart from one notable occasion on the Moon—an ill-fated 'romantic' evening with Julius Denisov involving champagne—she hadn't touched a drop of alcohol.

And she didn't see tonight as being anything different.

As Supervisor Mbemba whipped her around yet another corner, and deeper into the room which lay alongside the Banquet Hall, Alicia decided that if she was ever going to get any sort of answer on where they were headed—on what the big rush was about—then she would need to get it right now.

"Supervisor? Supervisor?"

Supervisor Mbemba jerked around. *"Refilwe,* please," she said, correcting Alicia.

Although Alicia would've normally taken a Supervisor chiding her to speak with her on first-name terms as a cause for celebra-tion, she couldn't quite muster enthusiasm this time around.

Despite her love of finding new experiences—of globe-trotting —she had never been the biggest fan of surprises.

Again, she supposed that her childhood farm-upbringing was to blame for that.

Wherever she was—whatever she chose to do—she supposed she would always, in one way or another, be a slave to routine.

Supervisor Mbemba—*Refilwe*—dragged Alicia on into what turned out to be a dead-end.

Alicia could clearly see that there was a pair of figures standing there.

Two *men* if she wasn't mistaken.

Why that was an issue, Alicia wasn't certain.

It wasn't like she was some Vestal Virgin.

The music was reduced to a mere *throb* of bass now, and Alicia imagined that this was the place where the more reckless of gamblers were brought when they seemed to be in need of calming down. For a heart-stopping moment, she was certain that Julius was one of the men, but she soon realised that the two silhouettes standing here were far *bulkier*—more *muscular*—than her former lover.

Refilwe spoke to the men in a language which Alicia recognised as being Afrikaans. Although she hardly spoke a word beyond, 'Hello'—*Hallo*—and 'Thank you'—*Dankie*—she could easily make out the cadence; the ebb and flow of the words. As she'd well learned throughout her travels, all languages had their own distinct flavour. Their own personality.

Finally, Refilwe turned away from the men, and, making to leave, she laid a steady hand on Alicia's shoulder. "Tomorrow," she said, "your services are likely to be required on one of the Shuttles. Will that be a problem?"

Alicia's gut dipped.

For a long few seconds, she struggled with this. Of course there was the will to *please* the Supervisor, to get her foot in the door by granting her request . . . but then there was *also* the practicality; the fact that she had to get working on those Mooncakes.

Before she truly had a chance to examine the problem from all angles, she found herself staring back into Refilwe's eyes; unable to resist.

She nodded in reply.

"Good," Refilwe said, with a smile as she left.

Alone with the men, now, Alicia looked them over again.

Although her eyes were still adjusting to the darkness, she realised that she *could* make out who one of the men was.

Patrick Fourie.

A South African pilot of one of the aforementioned Shuttles; the aerial vehicles put to use for more extensive—not to mention *hair-raising*—journeys across the surface of the Moon.

His hair was dyed in layered tones, ranging all the way from ochre to brunette, before finishing up in a much lighter blond shade. As with all the Shuttle pilots, he had a cool-eyed gaze, with a quiet sense of humour seeming to lurk beneath the surface at all times.

"Tomorrow," Patrick began, without delay, "we're planning to put on a picnic for the Thompson family at the North Pole. We thought that it might be a nice thing for us to serve them all warm apple pie." Here his mouth turned back at the corners. "And we thought, Supervisor Mbemba, and I, that it would only be appropriate for them to be served by a genuine *North American*."

Alicia waited out the pause in the conversation, realising that this could quite easily be her last chance to make her excuses and run. But, at the same time, she occupied herself on attempting to disentangle the identity of the other man; the one who was standing beside Patrick.

Her eyes had nearly adjusted now, though she continued to have trouble making out any defining features.

Realising a response was expected, she turned her attention back onto Patrick. "Actually," she began, "the thing is that—"

"Good," Patrick replied, smartly, succinctly. "Then I'll leave you in the company of Captain Zito—the two of you can thrash out all the details."

And, just like that, with a curt nod, Patrick was gone.

Leaving Alicia with the shock of just who she was standing here—*alone*—with.

Gofreddo Zito.

Son of the multibillionaire, technology mogul, Costantino.

It took Alicia another few seconds to fully clear her vision.

To adjust herself to the darkness.

Of course she had been caught up by the visitation of Gofreddo's father—*Costantino*.

Who hadn't been?

And—just as everyone else beneath the Dome—she had known of Gofreddo's desire to stay on beyond the allotted vacation period. Whereas his father, Costantino, had returned to Earth, Gofreddo had stayed behind. His father had no doubt pulled strings with Frau Köhler.

During her time travelling the world, Alicia had been somewhat taken aback at how easily the word 'Zito' rolled off the tongues of so many cultures. A synonym for the Zito Entertainment Units which bore his name.

The first aspect about Gofreddo which struck her was his square jaw. So much like his father's. It was just as she had seen in photographs. His blond hair stuck up in roguish tufts, and his eyes were a searing, sky-blue.

He looked the type who had been built for adventure, and, she couldn't help believing that the muscles beneath the tight-fitting tuxedo jacket, the permatan which covered his face, served only to confirm her theory.

"Gofreddo Zito," he said, outstretching his hand to her. "Pleased to meet you."

Alicia took it from him.

Felt his firm hold.

She didn't think to correct him that they had met previously . . . albeit *briefly*.

"Alicia," she said. "Alicia Brennan."

Rather than shake her hand up and down—as she was used to —he squeezed it, meeting her eyes with his smouldering gaze as he did so.

Alicia felt something within her melt.

She had heard all the stories. It was difficult to *avoid* the constant barrage of Gofreddo's likeness appearing on just about every media outlet across the face of the Earth. All those stories about what he was wearing, which events he'd recently attended, and, inevitably, who he was romantically involved with. If ever a reputation preceded someone, then it preceded Gofreddo Zito.

Finally, Alicia slipped her hand free of his. Not because she wasn't enjoying the skin-to-skin contact, which she was —*immensely*—but because she reminded herself of the larger game which was at stake here. That she was going through with this assignment in the hope of pleasing Supervisor Mbemba.

That was right.

Her *career*.

This was *all about* her career . . .

"So," Alicia said, feeling blood thumping to her temples now. "What's the plan for tomorrow?"

He didn't answer her, though. Instead, he reached out and pressed the back of his hand up against her forehead, as if taking her temperature. He pouted. "You look a little *flushed*," he said. "Are you feeling quite all right?"

A little taken aback to have this lovely specimen's hand draped across her forehead, Alicia took a couple of steps away. He seemed to get the message intuitively, removing his hand from her forehead at once. His pout eased into a smile.

"Yes, Gofreddo," she replied, belatedly. "I'm fine."

An awkward few moments passed.

The music seemed to grow louder—the bass thudded through the floor harder than before.

Finally it was Gofreddo who spoke. "I would like you to call me 'Fred', if that suits you."

"Actually," Alicia replied, amazed that she'd found her snark, "I think Gofreddo works better."

"I know what you have heard about me, and I just want to say, before you jump to any judgements, that you should have patience. That you should allow yourself to make your own mind up."

Here Alicia felt herself blushing again.

God, what she would've done for some kind of pill to stop that from happening.

She tilted her face slightly away from Gofreddo—'Fred'—hoping that she might be able to conceal her complexion from him. If he did notice then he had the social grace to ignore it this time, apparently not wishing to make her feel uncomfortable.

Alicia was glad for it.

Glad that he gave her space.

"I'll keep my mind open," she finally replied.

Gofreddo's eyes danced about their surroundings, over her shoulder. She thought that he was on the brink of excusing himself when he turned back to her at the last moment. "I am here, on the Moon, because my father struck a deal with Frau Köhler. Since they did business together—a shipment of bespoke entertainment units—she felt kindly disposed to my father's wishes.

"And when I informed my father that I would quite like to stay behind, to see how lunar life would suit me, he seemed only too happy to indulge me. He knows as well as you and I that back on Earth I have yet to find my place." He gave a shrug coupled with a pout. "That I have nothing there but parties, and occasions . . . and *dates*."

This final word, for some reason, sent a chill passing through Alicia's blood.

Almost as if he was *oversharing*.

Gofreddo continued, "I thought I might be able to discover some vocation on the Moon." Here an easy smile curled the corners of his lips. "And while I was here, I most certainly had my eye on the Shuttles . . . and now, lucky me, I get to pilot one."

"Yes," Alicia replied, without thinking, "lucky you."

Gofreddo held her gaze for a moment.

She half expected to feel the resentment pour off him, that bratty attitude to shine through from beneath. The disbelief that someone had the tenacity to criticise him—*the son of Costantino Zito!*

Instead, though, he only held himself firm. *Proud.*

Even though Alicia believed herself to be past all of that jealousy toward the rich—and the infinite opportunities which were the birthright of their offspring—she couldn't help her own background leaking out at times.

And Gofreddo surely wasn't any different.

He was just making the most of what the lucky roll of life had gifted him.

Finally, Gofreddo broke out into a wide, toothy grin. "All right," he said, "we shall see each other bright and early in the morning." And, with that, he walked away from her, heading back to whichever suite he was surely resident in back at the Lunar Grand.

Because people like Gofreddo Zito didn't *slum* it in the Basements with the rank-and-file . . .

4

REFLECTIVE ANALYSIS

*a*s *Gofreddo Zito* quietly lumbered away from the roaring party taking place in the Banquet Hall of the Stellar Tide Casino, he couldn't help but find his mind returning—over and over again—to that glorious creature he had had the pleasure of meeting this evening.

Who he had only now left behind.

Alicia Brennan.

That had been her name.

Those eyes, the colour of Braeburn apples, still struck him.

Made his heart thump just a few beats faster than normal.

Outside the Stellar Tide, he caught a PEAR back to the Basements. He recalled how, when he had first put the proposition to his father, that he should stay beneath the Celestial Stays Dome, he had wanted him to stay on at the Lunar Grand.

But Gofreddo would hear nothing of the sort. Although he might not have seriously entered upon any single career, or interest, never had to spend all that much time among a team of people working toward a common goal, he was well-versed on the subject of resentment; or as it was more lightly termed: *jealousy*.

Yes, he'd had to contend with that little devil throughout his life, from all those who envied him for simply who he was; for simply having been *born* Costantino Zito's child.

Although it was true that he had had all the luxuries he might've wished for growing up—that he'd never wanted for anything; not for a second—he wouldn't say it had been an easy childhood.

His father had done his best to give him a 'normal' upbringing, but that was rather difficult to achieve when seemingly on every street corner, lurking outside of the school gates, even, there were photographers watching and waiting to record his every waking—and sometimes *sleeping*—moment.

The attention hadn't ever let up—not for one second.

One thing was clear. Earth was waiting, with baited breath, to see just what Gofreddo Zito was going to do with his life; whether he was going to be a roaring success, or a crushing disappointment. For Gofreddo there could be no middle ground.

And although he had already plumbed the depths, and come up with several viable means to make his life the proverbial 'crushing disappointment', he had very few answers indeed when it came to the 'roaring success' eventuality.

Once he returned to his apartment in the Basements—no finer, and no lesser than any other employee's—he could once more feel the weight of expectation lying across the breadth of his shoulders. He had thought that by coming here—by *remaining* here—under the Celestial Stays Dome, he would be able to escape Earthly attentions. But, as he'd come to realise in the few weeks he'd been here as an employee, the worst of those attentions—the worst of those *pressures*—all came from within.

And yet, for those fleeting moments—the ones which he had spent in the company of Alicia Brennan—he had forgotten who he was. A brunette with a jagged haircut. A cute smattering of freckles, evenly distributed across either peach-toned cheek. And, above all else, an elegant, sleek figure which'd been all wrapped up by the blue-and-green tartan design of her dress.

He had played it cool, as he had long ago learned was the way.

Too many times he had been stung either by beautiful journalists looking for the inside scoop, or else those who would be easily swayed by the mere opening of pressmen's wallets. And he was determined not to let it happen again.

God, how he *wished* it wouldn't happen again.

Not with Alicia Brennan.

Because he had some *quite complex* plans for her.

5

CUSTOMISED ATTENTIONS

lthough it was true that she had an early start in the morning—what with accompanying the Thompson family and baking them a 'warm apple pie'—Alicia knew that there was no time to waste. She didn't even bother to return to the Basements to get changed out of her dress; she simply took a PEAR directly to the Orbital Café.

To her kitchen.

The faux-Alpine chalet was deserted. She wouldn't have any underlings coming in for several hours yet.

Once in the kitchen, she threw an apron over the top of her dress and set to work, mixing up the Mooncake recipe; knowing that she needed to get it right first time otherwise she wouldn't have a chance.

Sweat seeped out of her pores. It formed into beads and rolled down her cheeks. Every so often, she reached up and wiped it away with her forearm. After several hours of careful consideration—of mixing up ingredients and then setting them to bake in the oven—she turned her mind to the subject of the apple pie.

As she leaned up against the counter, well after four o'clock in the morning, she allowed herself a wry smile at the thought of switching her mind to the matter of the apple pie.

It was almost as if she was back to globe-trotting, if only in culinary terms.

It was almost seven in the morning by the time she'd finished up with her baking.

She took a quick taste test on both of her dishes. Although she didn't have what might've been described as a 'clean' palate, she had to admit that she'd done some tasty work indeed.

She placed the Mooncakes in the care of a nearby drone, then set the time and location for the delivery to the Wei family.

Once she'd got herself free of her apron, and was headed for the kitchen doorway, she found it blocked by a familiar—and *unwanted*—figure.

Julius Denisov.

He sniffed at the air.

"Smells good," he said.

Severely sleep-deprived, and knowing that she had to make every second count if she wanted to dip her head under a warm shower and get dressed in her Celestial Stays overalls, she was short with him.

"Out of the way," she said.

But he continued to stand in her path.

This time she met his eye.

He smiled wickedly at her.

"Didn't see you at the Stellar Tide last night," he said.

"Uh-huh," Alicia replied, backing away, preparing to rush at him if she needed to. "Well, I was there."

"Oh," Julius said, smiling wider still, "I know you were *there*. In fact, someone told me that you were keeping Gofreddo Zito company."

Seeing her opportunity, Alicia ran at Julius, aiming for a spot just below his ribcage, hoping that she might be able to wind him. But he was too quick for her.

He was several senses up on her.

Indeed, it felt as if her strength had gone.

She felt the urge to slap at his chest, as if that might convince Julius to move out of the way. As if it would make him see that he was being nothing short of an ass.

But, at the same time, she realised how futile it would make her seem.

How *weak*.

She couldn't help wondering if she should start to schedule some gym work so that she'd be well prepared for inevitable show-downs like these.

"Is that where you're going now?" Julius said. "To be with *Fred*?"

Although Alicia knew it shouldn't have done—although she knew that she had nothing to be ashamed of; except perhaps professional ambition—Julius's comment stoked a fury in the pit of her gut. It made her tingle all over.

"It's none of your business," she said, the words seething through her teeth. "Now get out of the way, or I'll have you reported!"

At this, Julius finally threw up his hands, turned side on, and allowed her to pass by. To leave the kitchen. She had only made it a couple of steps down the hallway, though, when she heard him calling back to her.

"Aren't you forgetting something?" he said.

Alicia stood stock-still.

She felt her heart beating up in her throat.

"I've instructed a drone to deliver the Mooncakes," she said, and then, feeling slightly sassy, added, "Do be kind enough to let me know what they think of them."

Again, she turned on her heel, leaving Julius behind.

But, once more, he called her back.

"Something else?" he said. "The apple pie?"

For a long few seconds, it felt as if her gut wound tighter and tighter. Blood fizzed through her veins, and up to her brain. It wasn't because he was getting to her—that he was getting the *better* of her . . . no, it was because he was right.

She *had* forgotten something.

She had left the apple pie in the oven when she'd intended to leave it to cool.

She toyed with the idea of leaving it behind—of forgetting all about it—but, in the end, she ventured back into the kitchen. Back past Julius, and she yanked the apple pie free of its place in the oven, depositing it down on a cooling rack.

That done, she made to leave again; glad to see that Julius was standing aside, apparently willing to let her free without opposition this time.

She already thought she'd made it out, and away, when he grabbed hold of her wrist. When he twisted it painfully, and whipped her around to face him. His eyes were almost like glowing coals, sunken in their sockets. His lips formed a pert, impossibly tight hole.

"You'll be sure to take care with that *dandy*, won't you, Alicia?"

Each word carried a sting to it.

She felt almost as if he had spit each one directly and deliberately into her eye.

It took all of her strength to keep from replying to him.

To keep herself from dropping down to his level.

She was patient. She waited for him to release her.

And, when he finally did, she stalked away.

Away from the kitchen—the place of her own which she'd always imagined safe.

As she stormed out of the side door of the Orbital Café, eyeing up a slowing PEAR, descending onto the landing pad, she heard his voice again from behind.

"Thanks for the Mooncakes, babe. Should go down a treat."

6

EXTREME ENTERTAINMENTS

*A*licia *sunk her teeth* into her lower lip.

She squeezed the arm rests of her chair tightly.

And, as Gofreddo Zito—or *Fred*, as he insisted she call him—pulled them into a fourth successive loop-the-loop, Alicia began to doubt if the chest and shoulder straps which held her in place were going to be able to resist the jarring forces.

Let alone her stomach.

As they flattened out, with the Thompson family whooping with glee behind, Alicia slipped Gofreddo, sat in the pilot's chair beside her, a scolding glance.

Just once—*just once*—she'd hoped that there might be a Shuttle pilot on the Moon who *didn't* think it was part of his job description to terrorise their passengers.

"All right," Gofreddo said, speaking through their earpieces, "we're closing on the landing site now—so don't go yanking off your restraints, or anything, okay?"

When Alicia turned around to take in the passengers—the

mother, father and the young boy; about nine—she couldn't see much past their beaming faces. It was impossible to deny that they had been tickled pink, first, to find that Costantino Zito's son would be flying their Shuttle and, second, that the Shuttle had turned out to be nothing short of a rollercoaster ride.

Despite guest satisfaction being decidedly at the top of any Celestial Stays employee's list of priorities, she couldn't help but wonder about the state of her apple pie following the breakneck aerobatics.

Gofreddo finally brought the Shuttle down to land on the North Pole. The Shuttle's legs bounced slightly as the articulated joints took the strain of the landing. He flipped off the thrusters, leaving the vital systems in place. With another flick of a switch, and the well-oiled sliding of gears, the Shuttle seating turned so that the chairs all faced into the centre.

Alicia was struck by the apparently endless lunar plains which swept out away from all sides of the Shuttle. Never before had she felt so alone, in all her life, as she did right now. As she peered upward, she made out the Earth, continuing to twirl away on its axis. Everybody she knew and loved was up there, waiting.

Waiting for her to come home.

Rolling his shoulders, no doubt getting shot of the pent-up tension which'd accompanied his aerobatics, Gofreddo clapped his hands together and grinned from ear to ear. "Who's ready for apple pie?"

The Thompson family cried with delight as one, and Alicia, feeling her legs shaking beneath her, undid her chest straps and staggered off into the back of the Shuttle.

She dug the box out from the storage bay. It was the standard piece of equipment she used to ship freshly baked goods. It was made of some synthetic white material which Alicia was loath to call 'plastic' and it had separate compartments so that individual portions could be pre-cut and stored securely, and freshly, awaiting consumption.

She carried the box back to the middle of the Shuttle, where the Thompsons' attention was one-hundred-per-cent focussed.

This morning, while she'd got herself washed up and dressed, she'd had one of her underlings venture back into the Orbital Café kitchens and box up the apple pie. They'd then sent it along in a drone to Gofreddo's Shuttle, and he'd duly loaded it on board.

Although Alicia knew that it was so *silly* to be so riled about how her cooking might turn out, she couldn't help but turn her mind back to another piece of advice her grandmother had given her; about how good food was quickly forgotten while great food, or, for that matter, *dreadful* food, was always remembered.

Despite taking a great deal of pride in the work she did beneath the Celestial Stays Dome, she couldn't help but feel that she would quite easily settle for a 'good' meal today.

Something nice . . . but forgettable.

As she opened the box, she took in the slices which'd already been laid out on paper plates, as per her instructions. Another function of the box was to maintain a certain temperature, and so she had instructed the pie to be kept 'pleasantly warm', and so satisfied Patrick Fourie's requirement of 'warm apple pie'.

Within the box was also provided milky coffee and hot chocolate.

She poured out their contents into paper cups with Mummy Thompson and Thompson Junior taking hot chocolate while Daddy Thompson predictably went for coffee.

Once she'd handed out the three slices pre-determined to be given to the Thompson family, and served them the coffee and hot chocolate, she turned her attention back downward, to the remaining two slices.

The slices which were intended for Gofreddo and herself.

Although there were many regulations surrounding what was considered to be 'fraternisation' between guests and staff—and sharing mealtimes, or similar, was one of these—Alicia knew when there was a line to be drawn; when she was better off using her intuition.

From her experience, whenever she found herself with guests, more or less alone, the guests tended to feel ill at ease if the staff didn't partake in whatever was being consumed. And this was something with which she could empathise. She could think of many occasions, when she'd been travelling through this country, or that one, when she'd found the owner, or manager of whichever establishment she happened to be frequenting an overbearing influence, looming over her as she ate, or drank, whatever they offered.

Being waited on, Alicia concluded, was an unnatural state.

Or, at least, one which she didn't—and would *not*—ever feel fully comfortable with.

And so she dished out Gofreddo's slice before digging into the box for her own.

When she brought her assigned slice out on its paper plate, she paused briefly, unable to take her eyes off the design which'd been scrawled out in icing upon the surface.

It was a love heart with the initials AB and GC written within.

"Everything okay?" Gofreddo said, from beside her.

Thinking quickly, she shielded her slice from him. And, before he could get a better look, she jabbed her fork into the icing. "Yes, fine," she said, forcing a smile.

Seeing that the Thompsons were staring at her too, she decided that she needed to be more emphatic in explaining away her response. "I thought there was a hair, but it was just a slight split in the pastry."

She watched on as the Thompson's mutual gaze switched almost instantly from concern to beady-eyed amusement.

When she turned back to her slice, though, she could still feel Gofreddo's gaze searing the side of her face. She wanted, more than anything, to tell him to mind his own business; to tell him to tuck into his own slice of apple pie . . . and, in the end, without the need for words, he seemed to get the message.

Loud and clear.

Once the apple pie and various beverages were done with, the Thompsons asked to return to the Dome.

Apparently this time choosing to use the grey matter between his ears, Gofreddo took it slow; not wanting any accidents on the way back since everybody's stomach was jammed full of apple pie.

When they settled down at Entry Clearance, ready to go back through all the rigmarole which accompanied an ingress or egress to the Dome, Gofreddo busied himself with the Thompson family, freeing them from their chest and shoulder straps.

All of them, a touch giddy, thanked Gofreddo for his services, and 'charming' company.

They also thanked Alicia a great deal for the warm apple pie they'd been served, and Alicia was only too glad to smile and nod along.

Once the Thompsons had departed the scene, Alicia allowed her facial muscles to relax, and a frown replaced what'd been her false smile.

She shifted off in the same direction the Thompsons had gone only for Gofreddo to call her back.

"Alicia?" he said.

She halted, wondering if she should just keep going. Those initials which'd been iced on top of her apple pie hung in her mind. As Julius's obvious involvement entered her thoughts, her hands formed fists down at her sides. She turned back to Gofreddo.

She took in that blond hair of his. She couldn't help wondering if he styled it to make it look like he'd just got out of bed, or if he was really that *au naturel* when it came to his appearance. She liked to believe the latter, though she was sure the former was closer to the truth. Men like him—*rich people*—didn't leave things to chance.

They dangled the world on a string.

She met his sky-blue eyes.

He gave her a wry smile. "Feeling a little queasy from the trip?"

And although it was a fact that she could feel her stomach tightening into a knot, she shook her head. "No," she replied. "It's just . . . I've got things to do—matters to attend to."

His smile widened for a fraction of a second into a toothy grin before scaling all the way back to a pout. "Well, don't allow me to hold you up. I know that there's an awful lot of work that needs doing beneath the Dome."

Just when she was certain that she'd offended him in some way, he flashed her another one of his winning smiles. And her heart bounced right up to her throat.

"Thanks for the ride," she said, turning on her heel, and leaving Gofreddo to do whatever he needed to do to his Shuttle.

Did Shuttles require hot waxing?

7

EARTHSIDE COMMS

*G*ofreddo *sat back* in his apartment, naked except for the towel which was wrapped about his waistline. Warm steam still plumed through the air from the shower he'd taken. It'd been quite a ride today. And that apple pie had been delicious. He couldn't help wondering what else Alicia Brennan might have up her sleeve; what other recipes she might be able to utilise in bringing delight to the masses.

Within his earpiece, the Link informed him that he had an Earthside request for communications. When he examined the note attached, he saw that it was his father, Costantino, who wanted to chat.

Gofreddo drew in a deep breath, and then sighed it out.

There were times when he was in the mood to speak with his father, and then there were the times when he would rather be alone. When he would rather be allowed to stew in his own thoughts. He wondered if there was anywhere within the realm of mankind where he might be afforded solitude—*time alone ...*

If there was any place like that then it certainly *wasn't* the Moon . . .

Or, at least, not beneath the Celestial Stays Dome.

Knowing that he'd only be in more trouble if he attempted to avoid the meeting, Gofreddo accepted the request, and his dynamic wallpaper soon switched to an enormous spread of his father's face. With a couple of blinks of the eye, he adjusted the aspect ratio so that his father didn't come across as menacingly humungous. Once he'd done so, he noted his father's study around him—the ceiling-to-floor bookshelves; and the large windows peering out across his father's vineyard just outside Salta, back home in Argentina.

His father wasn't alone.

Beside him sat a familiar lady.

The woman who he had met up here, beneath the Celestial Stays Dome, and who he had taken back down Earthside.

Wendy Flowme.

She had worked in the Crescent Gardens with Louise Williams; the girl who had been so kind as to take himself and his father beneath her wing for the duration of their vacation stay. Although he didn't feel much like smiling, Gofreddo aimed his grin at Wendy and greeted her with enthusiasm.

"*Buenas Tardes*," he said to her. He gave a nervous smile, and then gestured to himself, to his bare torso. "I apologise for being underdressed, if I had known that my father had company . . ."

But Wendy batted this observation away with a loose-wristed hand gesture. "I've seen men in far worse states than yours."

Gofreddo smiled back at her, and then cast his glance over them. He noted the sun streaming in through the windows of the study, and he could just make out the verdant pastures beyond; the horses dotting the field in the middle distance.

Feeling just a touch awkward to find himself facing up to his father's latest flight-of-fancy, Gofreddo turned his attention to making conversation. "You both look a little red-faced; have you been horseback riding?"

Almost as soon as he said it, Gofreddo noticed his error.

But it was too late now.

Wendy turned to his father, and his father turned into Wendy.

If at all possible, the two of them grew even more red-faced still.

Gofreddo couldn't help but give a wry smile; this time authentic. He clucked his tongue, and then said, "*¡Esta juventude tan loca!*"

When the two of them had gathered themselves back together, Wendy turned back to the camera, smiled, and said, "Well, I thought I would just say hi . . . now I'll leave the two of you to the father-son chat."

And, with that, she rose up out of her seat, and headed out of the study.

Gofreddo waited until the door had shut behind her before he addressed his father again, this time with a wagging-gesture which the two of them recognised as belonging to his father's *mamá*; to Gofreddo's *abuelita*.

Bedridden, she would be off in her room, at the far east wing of the house. As was normal, she would be attended to by Marta, their housekeeper who had been with them ever since Gofreddo was born. Soon Gofreddo imagined that Marta would take his *abuelita* out in her wheelchair to breathe some of the fresh afternoon air.

He thought of it as being somewhat wickedly ironic that while Marta had been employed to look after the infant Gofreddo, she had eventually ended up caring for a much older member of the family.

"I see that you have been giving her the *full* tour of the property. I wouldn't want to think that she didn't receive the *complete* experience."

Here Costantino blushed even further.

It was a point of entertainment—not to mention great pride—that Gofreddo could still manage to embarrass his father.

"So," Costantino said, "how've things being going up there? Are you still zipping about in those Shuttles?" He smiled, his normal colour returning to his face as the embarrassment apparently subsided. "Not broken any bones, I hope?"

Now it was Gofreddo's turn to blush.

But not for *romantic* reasons.

That afternoon, when he had been guiding the Thompsons across the lunar surface at breakneck speeds in his Shuttle, he'd been putting together the final pieces of the puzzle; attempting to get to grips with the intricacies of his plan . . . for the project which he would grow himself.

Something which he would build with his own hands.

He had been working on the project for months now—if not *years* subconsciously.

And his father would be able to shoot it down with a single syllable.

No.

"Father," Gofreddo said, feeling his voice crack a little under the heat of his gaze, "you remember how you've always said that you would be prepared to fund any venture which I put serious thought into? That you would be prepared to become an investor?"

Gofreddo's father's smile vanished. He tilted his head to one side, and shifted himself to the edge of his chair. He was the picture of seriousness now. "Yes?" he said.

"Well, I think I have found just the project."

"Hmm."

Throughout his life, Gofreddo had always seen his father as Costantino Zito—the great innovator and businessman. 'Father' had always seemed to be his secondary role.

Even from his earliest memories, Gofreddo could recall being extremely conscious of frittering away his father's time with childish japes.

But now, more than ever, it felt as if he couldn't waste so much as a word.

And so he just came out with it as clearly as he could.

"I would like to establish a production company on the lunar surface."

As Gofreddo had often witnessed his father, whenever someone put a large-scale business proposition to him, he leaned back in his chair and touched the tips of his fingers together. He remained like that, in silent consideration, for a good five minutes.

That was a long period of time even by his father's standards.

He usually remained silent for only half a minute; a *minute* at most.

Finally, his father turned his attention back to him. "I shall have to think about it," he said. "It would require a large outlay, not to mention some schmoozing of the relevant authorities—"

"Father," Gofreddo said, interrupting, "I have already thought through this. If we were to approach Frau Köhler she might be amenable to the idea. Think about the stars who would stay at the Celestial Stays Dome. Think about the publicity, not to mention—"

But his father waved away these comments.

Although he did it in a nonobtrusive way, smiling as he gestured, it didn't seem to reduce the sinking-heart feeling which passed through Gofreddo's entire body.

"I shall make my decision in a week's time," Costantino said.

Despite having yet more to blurt out to his father, all of these potential pitfalls which he had explored and wanted to counter before his father got a chance to bring them up himself.

But, as he well knew, that simply wasn't how Costantino Zito did business.

He would give his answer on the big picture alone.

And there was nothing Gofreddo could say or do to change his mind.

"Very well, father," Gofreddo said. "Then you shall give me your answer in a week?"

Still smiling broadly, Costantino held up his index finger. "One week," he replied, emphatically. "Now," he said, continuing, "since you've seen the state of my own love life, why don't you enlighten me as to how things are for you currently. *Romantically* speaking?"

Still reeling from having revealed his heart's desire, Gofreddo hardly had the courage to speak at any length on his personal relationships. But, as he well knew, for better or worse, if Gofreddo was to continue pursuing Alicia Brennan then his father would find out sooner or later.

Gofreddo, after all, was always being watched.

8

PROXIMITY ALERT

*a*licia *stormed past* the backgammon tables. She breezed by the pontoon. And she tore along the endless row of slot machines, knocking over a vacated stool as she went on her way.

When she reached the double doors which separated the main floor of the Stellar Tide Casino from the staff-only area, the member of Security standing there had the good sense not to try and stop her; to press her for credentials.

Before she knew it, she was stomping her way up the spiral stairs which led to Julius Denisov's office. As she leaped the final step, she tuned into Julius's voice. She could hear him conversing with someone or other. It didn't matter. She was determined to have an explanation for what had gone on earlier that day.

How *dare* he sabotage her apple pie.

How *dare* he scribble those initials in icing on her slice.

Just *who* did he think he was?

Without pausing, she marched in through the doorway of Julius's office.

She spied him, in his articulated chair, his back to the landscape of the Celestial Stays Dome sweeping out behind him. He was dour-faced, his hands clutched on the desk before him. His skin seemed so pale compared to Gofreddo's—his body almost *lanky*—and Alicia couldn't think what she'd *ever* seen in him.

When his eyes swept up onto hers, and his lips parted slightly in shock, she gave him no chance to get so much as a *squeak* out past his throat.

She grabbed hold of the collar of his overalls, squeezing as tightly as she could.

In that moment she was certain she could've choked him to death.

It felt like she possessed the required strength.

As his eyes bulged from their sockets, Alicia heard a strong voice of reprimand at her heels. But she didn't halt. This was between her and Julius, and she couldn't really care less who found out about what he'd done to her . . . how he'd attempted to humiliate her in front of Gofreddo.

"Why?" she said, her voice raspy gravel. "*Why* did you do it?"

But Julius's eyes slipped free of her own, and turned to look over her shoulder.

She gave him a shake.

"*Look at me*! I thought you couldn't get *enough* of me . . . isn't that why you keep on hanging around the kitchens? Isn't that why you can't leave me *alone*?"

"Alicia!"

Again, it was the voice of reprimand at her heels.

Still, she didn't turn around.

She was intent on getting a response from Julius.

One way or another, she wanted to find out the answer to her question.

She wanted all this to stop.

"*Answer me!*" she said, this time with her voice breaking.

She felt close to tears.

But she forced them back down, into the corners of her eyes.

She thought back to all the times when she had been travelling alone. And when she had wanted to cry. She had only recalled her grandmother's words; recalled what her grandmother had said to her on her deathbed:

We're never really alone. Not when we have our memories. Not when we have our imagination. Not when we have inner strength.

Alicia drew on that inner strength now.

That inner *steel*.

Before Julius could gather any words at all together, Alicia felt the firm grip on her shoulder. She gave herself up to the brute force, feeling her own physical strength deserting her. It took her only a couple of moments to note the flowing red hair, and the laser-green eyes. As she was completing her fact-finding gaze, she noted the golden Supervisor's patch sewn onto the breast pocket.

Mackenzie Angliss.

Supervisor Mackenzie Angliss.

In charge of the Human Resources Division.

"Just what is the *meaning* of this?" Mackenzie said, running her words together in her strong Australian accent.

Alicia felt numb.

A prickling sensation passed over the surface of her skin.

She thought about her actions—about what she'd just done.

She'd acted like a nut.

And yet it'd seemed the only way to blow off steam.

Alicia took a deep breath, feeling Mackenzie's long manicured fingernails digging into her shoulder. She did her best to appear calm, as if she had this situation under control. As if she hadn't just burst in here, moments ago, like some loon.

She nodded in Julius's direction. "He knows what this is about."

Mackenzie met Alicia's eye, and looked over to Julius. "What *is* this about?" she said.

Smoothing out his collar from where Alicia had seized hold of him, she could tell that he was trying to make out that he was not only unflustered by the episode, but also blameless.

With a pout and a vague shrug, he said, "I have no idea."

Mackenzie's focus shifted back to Alicia. "Brennan," she said, her pronunciation of Alicia's surname stinging slightly considering that Alicia had always considered herself and Mackenzie, if not friends, then very good acquaintances, "you have no authorisation to be here. Can you find your own way out, or do I need to call Security?"

Alicia fired a stare off at Julius again.

She felt an almost stabbing urge in her gut to fly at Julius's throat. Julius seemed to sense this as he physically retreated back into his chair. But Alicia held herself together.

She wouldn't allow her temper to dominate.

She switched her attention back onto Mackenzie.

"You're relieved of your duties with immediate effect pending inquiry. You are to return to your room to await further instruction."

It felt almost as if a hollow was forming within Alicia's chest.

As if the spot where her heart had once been was gone.

Replaced only by a neutral unfeeling void.

"Is that understood, Brennan?"

Alicia met Mackenzie's brilliant green eyes.

Gave a doleful nod.

"Good," Mackenzie replied, then added, "I'll trust you to leave of your own accord."

Alicia lingered for another few seconds, and then, after firing off a parting stare in Julius's direction so as not to lose face, she strode out of the office, back down the spiral stairs, and boarded a PEAR waiting on the landing strip outside the Stellar Tide Casino.

9

EMPATHETIC RESPONSE

Having no further orders, other than the one which condemned her to her room back in the Basements, Alicia was forced to abandon the Orbital Café for the rest of the shift; leaving it in the hands of her underlings.

It was the worst situation imaginable.

She could recall the last time, about a month or two ago, when, through sickness, she had been unable to go through with her shift. She had managed no more than a day of bedrest before she'd felt compelled to return . . . and it'd been a good thing she had too.

When she'd arrived to the kitchen, the whole place had been a *mess*.

Although she would've forgiven her staff for breaking with her own policy of hand-cleaning the kitchen, she returned there to find that her staff hadn't so much as set a *droid* to clean the place. She recalled walking a few steps in through the kitchen door only to near enough break her neck when she'd slipped on a puddle of spilled milk. In the end she'd only been saved by the blob of treacle which'd given her some much needed balance.

As she lay herself down on her bed, Alicia's imagination began to get the better of her; thinking through all of the various scenarios—mainly involving the distinct smell of burning pastry.

When she could take lying down no longer, she forced herself up onto her feet and began to pace from one end of the room to the other like a caged panther.

When the Link informed her—via her earpiece—that she had a visitor waiting outside her door, she expected the very worst. While she'd been waiting, she'd even imagined the scenario of Karolin Köhler herself turning up outside her door; having travelled to the Moon to personally fire her before escorting her back to Earth.

Alicia had no idea what'd got into her.

She was usually so good at keeping her true thoughts and feelings all bundled up within.

What was it that'd got her so feisty? Did she *really* care all that much about how she appeared in Gofreddo's eyes? Did she *really* care whether or not Julius embarrassed her in front of him?

The Link informed Alicia, as she padded to the door, that her visitor was not Karolin Köhler, but, in actual fact, Louise Williams.

Perhaps this was how Celestial Stays had decided to break the news to her; perhaps they believed that she was less at risk of freaking out if her closest friend was the one to tell her to take her coat and head back Earthside.

Louise looked a touch concerned as she trod into the room, but, from what Alicia could tell, there was no sign of a Security escort accompanying her. That didn't mean that they weren't being watched very closely, however. After her display at the

Stellar Tide, Alicia could hardly blame Celestial Stays for taking the cautious approach.

Louise attempted a slight smile, and, against all odds, Alicia found the strength to smile back at her. "Want to go for a walk in the Gardens?" she said.

"I'm under house arrest," Alicia replied, dryly.

Louise shook her head. "I've got special permission— Mackenzie herself told me that I should come and see how you're doing . . . see if I could get to the bottom of what's going on."

Alicia blinked slowly several times. "So I'm not getting canned?"

Louise shrugged. "Not from what I've heard. Not *right away*, in any case."

"That's reassuring," Alicia replied, her response caked in sarcasm.

"Come on," Louise said, reaching out and taking hold of Alicia's arm by the crutch of her elbow. "A little wander among the flowers'll do you a world of good."

Alicia had to admit that the 'wander among the flowers' made her feel infinitely better.

It seemed to cleanse her mind; to wipe her thoughts free of Julius's smug, snub-nosed, pale face.

As she went through everything that'd happened with Louise, she felt almost as if she was having a weight eased off her shoulders. It felt so good to share her problems; to allow someone else to take the burden for a change . . . and to have someone who understood, from personal experience, all about controlling men; the ones who just *refused* to let go when the love was clearly gone.

When they reached the end of the Crescent Gardens, and found themselves standing reverent with the Earth twirling away above their heads, Alicia felt as if she was approaching something like her normal self.

"It's just," she said, with a slight sigh to her voice, "Julius thinks he can come rushing into my kitchens at any time of his choosing; so why shouldn't I be able to go and tread all over his office when *I* feel like it?"

Louise met her eye for a moment, and then glanced off to the edge of the Dome. As she stared out across the lunar plains, her voice took on a slightly floaty quality. "What you've got to remember is that the second you make it a game he's won."

"A 'game' ?" Alicia replied. "Who said this was a *game*? If Mackenzie hadn't stopped me back in the Stellar Tide, I was just as likely to have scratched the bastard's eyes out."

Louise smirked. "And that was probably the least of what he deserved."

"Tell me about it," Alicia said, folding her arms across her chest.

"Sometimes, though, we've got to avoid bringing ourselves down to *their* level."

"Whose level?"

Louise eyed her closely. "*Men's.*"

"Oh."

"Having said that," Louise went on, now casting her gaze back across the gardens, and—Alicia noted—to Njhay as he emerged from the laboratories, "once we make it a game the only way to win is by playing to our own strengths."

"And what're those?"

"*Cunning,*" Louise said, counting on her fingers. "Bravery. Dignity. Dutifulness"—Louise was coming to her thumb now —"And, above all else, *Patience.*"

60

" 'Patience' ?" Alicia replied. "You mean that it wasn't the best game plan for me to try and scratch his eyes out?"

Louise shrugged. "All you did was give him the attention that he's so sorely craving. If you starve him of that attention, pass him off as meaning nothing at all, then he'll soon grow bored and go bother some other poor girl."

"That's sage advice," Alicia said.

Louise arched an eyebrow. "And speaking of sage advice, you should get going on bothering another man of your own."

She nodded off in the direction of some bristling, twirling tulips.

Just over the top of them, Alicia made out a familiar figure.

Gofreddo Zito.

Her heart thumped up in her throat.

She turned back to Louise. "What happens now?" she said. "Have I been demoted? Have I been unceremoniously shifted away from the Orbital Café?"

"A verbal warning," Louise replied, matter-of-factly. "That was how Mackenzie told me you were supposed to treat this."

Alicia nodded. "Sounds fair," she said. "And I can return to normal duties tomorrow?"

"Yep," Louise said, and then, unexpectedly patting Alicia on the buttocks, she added, "Go get him."

It was only as Alicia drew closer to Gofreddo that it struck her that this might not be the ideal time. He walked with his head bowed, clutching his chin, his gaze firmly fixed on the brick path. He seemed to be almost unaware of just where he was—that he was walking in the Crescent Gardens at all. As he trudged along, he spoke to himself in Spanish. And although Alicia's Spanish comprehension was proficient, she struggled slightly to get to grips with his Argentine dialect.

She might've stood a greater chance if he'd spoken loud enough for her to make out the words clearly; but he was only talking to himself.

Alicia was on the point of turning around, returning to the Basements, when she shifted a glance over her shoulder. She saw Louise, now being embraced from behind by Njhay, staring intently at her; clearly imploring her to close the gap.

To bag her this prime specimen of man flesh.

With a quick sup of air, Alicia turned back, trod her way up to Gofreddo, then said, "Hi."

Gofreddo flinched at her word, as if he might've been half expecting a mugger to leap out from behind one of the bushes. When he recognised her, however, his expression shifted from weary surprise to a thick-lipped smile.

"Hello," he said. "Fancy seeing you here."

"It's a nice place to spend the afternoon."

"I find it that way," he replied, with a gentle smile, turning his gaze to the flowers which surrounded them.

Alicia cast a quick glance back over her shoulder, to Njhay and Louise, realising that they'd departed the scene, walking hand in hand, heading in the direction of the laboratories.

Alicia's overactive imagination couldn't help but conjure an idea of what they might be about to get up to . . .

She shifted her attention back to Gofreddo. "You look like you've got something on your mind."

Gofreddo seemed slightly startled. He parted his lips, but, at first, no sound came out. Then, finally, his easy familiar smile returned. "What makes you say that?" he said.

"Well, you're walking about here—*alone*—and you're talking to yourself."

"Ah," he replied, his smile slipping slightly. "Yes. I can see that you're an expert in human psychology."

"What's the matter?" she said.

Gofreddo stared back into her eyes.

Alicia felt her heart wrench in her chest.

A chill entered her blood.

And her stomach sank.

Those searing blue eyes of his had peered out from so many media outlets. Because the image of them was so embossed on her mind's eye, it seemed almost as if this was a living dream coming true. She supposed this was the reason why Gofreddo was so wary around strange women. He had seen their reaction to him from the outside so many times—and he knew how it might make them vulnerable. But, then again, he'd never met a woman like Alicia.

"Oh," Gofreddo replied, breaking off eye contact, "it is just something between myself and my father."

"You're not fighting, are you?"

He shook his head. "No, that's not it." He smiled warmly. "My father and I, we never fight. My father does not believe in it."

"Is that so?"

"Hmm."

Alicia decided that it was better for her to drop the topic of conversation for the time being. She didn't want to make Gofreddo think that she *was* intentionally trying to sniff out some juicy gossip that she could later sell to the media.

. . . What *did* she want?

When she glanced back over the flowers, she saw that Njhay and Louise had completely disappeared from sight now; and that, consequently, she and Gofreddo were just as alone as they were ever going to be beneath the Celestial Stays Dome.

There might not be a better time than now.

And when had she ever been the one to shy away from taking the initiative?

Gofreddo was staring at one flower in particular when he realised how intently she was staring at *him*. He seemed slightly taken aback. Once more, he parted his lips, ready to say something, but this time Alicia didn't give him a chance.

She pressed her lips up *hard* against his own.

To begin with, he retreated.

For a heart-stopping moment, Alicia was certain he was going to pull away.

But he remained there.

Pushing back against her.

As he kissed her deeper and deeper, as his tongue burrowed into her mouth, she moved her hands up his chest, bringing them eventually to rest on his pectoral muscles. When she dug in her fingernails, they were just as hard as they had looked when she'd first set eyes on them, beneath his tuxedo at that party.

When they finally broke apart, Alicia thought Gofreddo's eyes sparkled.

Or maybe it was just the arrangement of the lighting.

But it stirred something in her all the same.

And she wondered if she had ever felt exactly this way.

She certainly couldn't remember a time.

"Well," Gofreddo said, his fingers lightly tracing her own, "that was *very nice*."

" 'Very nice' ?" Alicia said, a flash of rage passing through her; perhaps a remainder of the anger she'd felt toward Julius that afternoon.

If Gofreddo sensed the fury then he made no reaction.

Smiling warmly with that dewy look in his eyes.

Alicia forced herself to calm down. She allowed the chill to enter her blood. "Would you like to try again?"

"Yes," Gofreddo replied, leaning into her. "Very much."

CLEAN-UP CALL

A licia *peered out* through the PEAR's visor, at the lunar plains rapidly disappearing below her. She could just about make out her reflection in the glass. And she was some-what surprised to note that she was *smiling*. Even when she noticed, she couldn't stop herself. And just like that—as simple as a *snap* of the fingers—she was being cast back to yesterday evening when she'd stood in the Crescent Gardens with Gofreddo.

The kiss they'd shared.

The warmth passing between them.

The union of two souls . . .

Okay, okay, now she was getting carried away.

Sure, it'd been a hot making-out session—the hottest she'd had for some time; if not *ever*—but she was no longer some giddy adolescent, sticking her tongue out like some farmer's dog in heat. Then again, it was all very well saying that, but did it make it the truth?

Could she really claim that she *wasn't* caught in the snares of Gofreddo Zito's charms?

To think that the two of them had parted before finishing what they'd started made her heart sink slightly. But only for a moment. Soon it leaped back into action, skipping free as her imagination whipped up numerous, scandalous scenes and situations playing out between her and Gofreddo.

One thing was for certain, if they *were* going to play at being dogs, then she was determined to be the one to make Gofreddo *beg*.

The PEAR swooped down on the Orbital Café, finally coming to rest on the landing pad. As she stepped out of the PEAR, her mind returned to practicalities; to real-world, everyday concerns.

A long way from romance . . . or, well, whatever *the hell* that kiss had been.

As she reached up to tuck a strand of hair behind her ear, she thought it something of a minor miracle that the café was even still standing. Her steps were plodding as she made her way up the path to the front door. The foreboding had already begun. Before she'd even set foot inside.

Could she smell smoke lingering on the air?

That unmistakable, distinctive odour of burning baked goods?

As was her wont, she first paid a visit to the customer section of the café; noting the wooden beams which hung down from the ceiling, and the animated open fireplace which gave off realistic warmth. She dwindled a few times on the little pieces of miscellanea: the oxygen tanks, the gauges and dials, the spacewalk suit which stood up near the entrance of the café like the modern-day equivalent of a suit of armour in a medieval castle.

'Kitsch' didn't even begin to describe it, in truth.

But after all this time—all the *love* Alicia had invested in the place—she could at least admit that it carried a homey quality; even if it was just in Alicia's own eyes.

There were no guests waiting to be served, which was a mercy, so she passed on into the kitchens, preparing herself mentally for the dreadful sight about to face her.

She stood in the doorway. And she was surprised to find that the entire kitchen was still in one piece. There wasn't even a trace of the smoke which she had breathed in from outside. Perhaps it had just been her imagination, after all.

She eyed the three members of staff who were working under her that day, taking them all in, one by one. Finally, her gaze fell on another member there—someone who was out of place; someone who didn't belong in the kitchen of the Orbital Café.

Her sleek, dark-brown hair was tucked neatly into a businesslike ponytail. Her eyes were such a deep oak colour that Alicia could've sworn that they were black. And her skin, she couldn't help noticing, was a flawless hazelnut tone.

Although Alicia had seen her around before, she had to read her nametag to jog her memory: K. SINGH. And then she recognised the Indian flag which was sewn onto the breast pocket of her overalls . . . a Guardian's badge, too.

Feeling somewhat bemused now, Alicia shifted her attention upward, to K. SINGH's eyes. She was taken aback to note that she was smiling at Alicia.

"Hello," she said, her voice thick with the soft, accented English Alicia had grown so familiar with during her travels in India.

Alicia opened her mouth to speak, and then clamped her lips shut all over again. "I . . . I . . ." she finally managed to get out.

"It's Kyra," K. SINGH—*Kyra*—said.

"Oh, uh . . . *Alicia*."

Kyra gave her a wide grin filled with perfectly aligned, pearl-white teeth.

Alicia felt an odd jabbing sensation at the base of her spine. Her heart throbbed in her chest. She wondered if she was still recovering from the anger which'd coursed through her body the day before, when she'd gone for Julius at the Stellar Tide. It brought her out in a flush even to think about it now with a relatively cool head.

What'd got into her?

She used to be so good at controlling herself.

At keeping her *animal* instincts well and truly buried.

Deep down.

Feeling as if somebody had delivered a punch to her temple, Alicia turned back to Kyra. "What . . . what is this?" she said.

"Oh," Kyra said, batting a hand, "Mackenzie Angliss wanted to have a Guardian looking over things here, while you were"—she paused, tellingly—"*away.*" Kyra's smile dialled down a couple of notches in intensity. "You left really great instructions. It was just a case of babysitting, really."

" 'Babysitting' ?" Alicia repeated.

"Uh-huh, just making sure that the café didn't burn down—something like that."

Alicia took in the kitchen for the first proper time, bringing the blurry image clearer. *Cleaner.*

There was Millat, delivering a whole tray of croissants into an oven, where they would stay, kept to a gently warm temperature in case they were ordered by the clientele.

The white apron was tied neatly behind his back, and his matching, white paper hat perched neatly on his well-combed hair. He gave Alicia a nervous smile when their eyes crossed, as if what he was doing was akin to some kind of mutiny.

Taking orders from someone *else*.

But Alicia thought nothing of the kind.

She was simply *bowled-over* that the whole kitchen hadn't descended into complete and utter chaos; the precursor to a smouldering pile of ashes.

She looked to Stéphanie, standing at the sink. Like Millat, she wore the apron—the white paper hat. She was hand scrubbing pots and pans clean; just as Alicia liked the job to be done. She always believed that the droids had a tendency to break far more than was necessary. More often than not, it took a caring, human hand, to keep the crockery from damage.

Next, her gaze instinctively fell on Drake, from Ghana, and just into his early twenties. He had a tendency to be lacking when it came to the details—when there were delicate touches, such as icing, to be done. As she zoned in on his current task, as he went about glazing a whole tray of Chelsea buns prior to being placed in the oven, he didn't seem to even notice her. With his forehead wrinkled, he remained focussed on his work.

Stunned, Alicia turned back to Kyra. "Uh, thank . . . you," she said, at last.

"Don't mention it," Kyra replied, her smile at least as brilliant as it had been before.

Alicia remained standing beside her, the two of them surveying the busy employees working around them for what must've been longer than ten minutes. Neither of them spoke. Alicia, at least, was spellbound by the activities being carried out without her needing to utter so much as a word. Right then, for the first time since she had taken over the administration of the Orbital Café, she wondered if she'd been putting too much pressure on herself.

If she'd been placing too much *importance* on herself.

Because, sure, she had been the one to put all of these recipes together in the first place, but now that her employees knew what to do, was it really necessary that she be so intense in her supervision? The answer seemed to be *no*.

A falling baking tray—accompanied by a metallic *twang!*—brought Alicia back to reality.

She blinked away her daze, and saw that, while washing up, Stéphanie had let slip the baking tray, and that it'd fallen at her feet.

Red-faced, and casting a glance back at Alicia, Stéphanie bent down to retrieve the tray. Lipping a silent apology, she turned her attention back to the washing up.

Alicia allowed herself to exhale.

Well, things weren't *quite* perfect.

There was still room for improvement.

Finally, feeling as if an uneasy tension had tightened in the air between herself and Kyra, Alicia turned to her and said, "Thanks for your help—I should be able to take things from here."

Kyra remained where she was. Unmoved.

Alicia stared back at her.

Kyra's smile loosened a touch. "Mackenzie told me that I should stay around here for a while, just to—"

"*Spy* on me?" Alicia replied, her voice straining.

Kyra's gaze slipped away from Alicia's.

She seemed to want to focus on just about anything else.

Alicia looked back over the kitchen, then breathed out a sigh. "Well," she said, "at least you've been holding the fort nicely."

Although Alicia was somewhat riled—to put it mildly—about how Mackenzie Angliss had dropped a spy into the Orbital Café, she was surprised at how quickly she forgot entirely about Kyra's presence there.

She kept things tight with her staff, supervising their baking, offering advice, encouragement, and reprimand, in even bursts among them. As always, she set herself to tending to front of house; to actually serving the customers.

Before allowing anything out of the kitchen, she gave it a taste test, ensuring that the sweetening was up to scratch or that the texture was *just so* . . . and she was surprised to find that her employees had done such a great job.

She wondered if that made her a bad boss.

Did it reflect badly on her own management to expect so little of her employees?

Why was it that she always wanted to control every *last* thing in her life?

. . . It was almost a return to her former childhood self.

Midway through the afternoon, Louise popped into the Orbital Café. As she sat down at one of the tables with a view looking out across the lunar plains, she removed the mud-caked gloves she'd been wearing that morning for her work in the Crescent Gardens.

"Sit," Louise said, nodding to the chair opposite.

Although Alicia would've normally refused such a request, never wanting to be found *sitting* when some crisis or other was going off, she decided that, based on what she had discovered about the Orbital Café that morning—and, to a larger extent, *herself*—she could afford to take five minutes with her best friend.

"So," Louise said, "How'd it go?"

Alicia smirked. "How'd *what* go?"

"The date."

"It wasn't a *date*."

Louise rolled her eyes. "Well, how'd the *not*-date go?"

Alicia held herself still.

Just to think about her meeting with Gofreddo the night before sent her heart pitter-pattering up her throat. All the muscles in her body seized tight for a long moment, and then, when she urged them to do so, lest she pull something vital, they relaxed.

"It was," Alicia belatedly replied, "*interesting*."

Louise leaned over the table, propping herself up on her elbows. " 'Interesting' *how*?"

"Well, he was, uh, I don't know . . . I guess you'd say that he was taken by surprise."

"But in a good way?"

Alicia studied this question for several seconds.

And then decided.

"Yes," she said. "I'm fairly certain it *was* a good way."

Louise grinned, then glanced about the café.

For a heart-stopping moment, Alicia was certain that she was going to point out that Gofreddo was nearby; that he was within earshot.

But when Alicia looked around there were only two tables occupied, as had been the case earlier.

Moreover, all the guests were far too occupied in finishing off their pastries and hot beverages to pay any attention to the two members of the Celestial Stays staff seated off to one side of the room.

Louise sank back into her chair, giving Alicia some much-needed relief.

It felt better not to have Louise pressuring her for 'details'.

"So," Louise continued, her tone casual, though the deliberate way she picked dried-on mud from her gloves was anything but, "when're you seeing him again?"

Alicia breathed in deeply, feeling the air filling her lungs.

Her stomach sank slightly.

Then she gazed back out of the window, across the lunar plains.

"We haven't set a date yet," she said.

Louise arched an eyebrow, still considering her muddied gloves. "Well, I'd get a move on, if I were you . . ." She glanced up at Alicia. "A man like that—a man of Gofreddo Zito's . . . *calibre*—won't stay on the market for very long."

Now it was Alicia's turn to smirk. "And what was all that advice you were dishing out before, you know, about 'patience' and 'dignity' . . . all that?"

Louise screwed up her eyes. "Now, come on, Ally, you're a woman; you should be able to work it out . . . you can be all of those things and, at the same time, be *insistent*."

" 'Insistent' ?"

"Yuh," Louise replied, flashing her eyebrows. "I mean," she continued, turning back to picking the dried mud from her gardening gloves, "you're a successful woman—you've done well to end up looking over the only café on the entire Moon. Surely when you see something you want, you *take* it."

Here, for some reason, Alicia felt herself grow a touch faint.

When she spoke again, her voice was weak.

Frail almost.

"What if some things . . . what if they *can't* be controlled?"

"What're you talking about?"

Alicia stared back into Louise's eyes for several moments, and then shifted her attention to the lunar plains surrounding them. "I just mean that you can't, you know, control everything. I know because I . . ."

"Because you what?"

Alicia snapped back onto her.

Her mind felt strangely sharp.

"Never mind," Alicia said. "It doesn't matter."

Louise frowned. "If you say so." She glanced about the café, and then back to Alicia. "Right," she said, "I'd better be off." She gave a wry smile. "And don't you forget to fill me in on all the details—all the info about this *Gofreddo* character . . . I'll never forgive you if I end up reading about it in the media, okay?"

Alicia tried her best to chuckle at this remark, but it merely died in her throat.

Louise didn't seem to notice as she got up and wandered away.

As Alicia stared out across the lunar plains, she couldn't help but feel herself being swept back into the past; going back to those . . . *painful* times . . . the times that she had believed long past; the times that she thought she had forgotten long ago.

The *pain* she believed she'd escaped.

"Um, excuse me?"

Alicia glanced up, saw that one of the guests was calling to her; clearly wanting to order something else. She reached up to her cheeks and was surprised to find that they were damp.

Tears.

Before she turned back to the guest, and to his wants, she wiped her cheeks dry with her palms.

Back to work.

Time to get back to work.

11

PARENTAL APPROVAL

*I*t was *precisely* a week later when Gofreddo received the notification that his father wished to speak with him.

And although he had been expecting the meeting—been *anticipating* it ever since his father had set the date—he found that the thought of it had turned him into something like a nervous wreck.

He'd decided to take care of the muzzle which'd grown out of his face over the past couple of days. He used an old-style, non-electrical razor. In fact, it was an antique. It had once belonged to his grandfather. The handle was made of a polished bull's horn which had slowly begun to turn yellow about the edges. And although his technique was usually flawless—just as his father himself had taught him—this morning, he simply couldn't manage to keep the blade straight and he gave himself a pair of nicks beneath the chin.

Once he'd blotted the cuts with some toilet roll, he paced his room—back and forth, back and forth—waiting for the inevitable notification from his father to come through.

Still shaking, although he hoped not visibly, Gofreddo took his place on the edge of the bed, and brought his father up on his dynamic wallpaper.

Unlike the time before, his father was alone . . . there was no sign of Wendy.

And, despite his father's ever-present smile, he couldn't help but believe that a certain sadness lurked just behind his eyes. A sadness which he hoped to hide, but which Gofreddo—as his son, and the person who arguably best knew him in the world—could detect without too much trouble.

Deciding to fix his mind onto the most logical cause, Gofreddo immediately brought up the subject of Wendy. His father informed him that Wendy had returned to her native Zimbabwe following the visit. And since he didn't intimate that she would be back at any time in the near future, Gofreddo was fairly confident he had pinned down the cause for his father's melancholy.

Gofreddo wasn't entirely sure what to make of all this.

So he decided to just stay quiet.

Although he had more than his share of experience in the ways of love—in the ways of *relationships*—he wouldn't ever presume to be better at judging anybody else's matters from the outside. And least of all his *father's* . . .

Gofreddo waited for his father to bring up the topic they'd discussed the week before, concerning the production company on the Moon. He knew that this was the way his father did business. *He* needed to be the one who was in control.

And, sure enough, his father did bring it up.

"Now, son, about this proposal of yours." His father stared into the camera with steady determination; unshifting concentration.

Gofreddo knew from having witnessed his father conducting many different business meetings through a screen that he would never—*ever*—attempt to multitask. Gofreddo recalled a time when he had directly asked his father about this, and he had informed him that, aside from the disrespect it showed his prospective business partner, it meant that he closed off a great deal of his brain power when most needed.

It was just as important to pick up on the non-verbal signals as it was the *actual* verbal ones being spoken through the lips.

What might his father be garnishing about him now?

Gofreddo was certain his father must've noted his shaking.

"I've had time to think," his father continued. "And I am willing to grant it the go-ahead, with certain caveats."

The warm feeling started slowly—right in the centre of Gofreddo's chest—but it soon entered his blood and began to flow steadily about his body. He felt the warming sensation passing to the extremities—to the very tips of his toes and fingers. When the sensation reached his head, the effect was almost giddying.

He thought he might faint.

Yeah, it was better that he didn't do that.

Not right now . . .

He turned his mind back to the conversation, sure that his father had noted the unspoken glee which'd just spread through him. "What are the caveats, father?" Gofreddo asked.

His father remained still for several moments, not answering.

Gofreddo got to wondering if his father was going to change his mind.

If—at the last possible moment—he was going to switch his opinion.

But, as it was, he continued. "As you know, your *abuelita* has been unwell for quite some time."

Gofreddo was taken off-guard by this change of direction in

the conversation. And it was only then that he realised his error; that he had neglected to ask after his *abuelita's* health, as he almost always did at the beginning of any conversation with his father.

Although he would never put so much into words, it was a great source of pride for Gofreddo to think that since his father worked from home he could spend such a great deal of time with his infirm mother; Gofreddo's *abuelita*.

"While Wendy was here," his father continued, "I decided to introduce her to *Abuelita*." Here his father's cheeks flushed slightly, but not with shame, more with a sense of humour, if his wide smile was any sort of evidence to go by. "The two of them hit it off very nicely indeed, what with Wendy telling her all about the Moon—about the Celestial Stays Dome up there." His father suddenly became more sombre. "I remember when you were a little boy, you used to ask me all the time about my father—about your *abuelito*—wanting to know what had happened to him." His father dropped his voice even further now. "It was always difficult, because your *abuelita* was so insistent that you were not to know the truth. That you were not to know about the *tragedy*."

Gofreddo screwed up his brow. "What 'tragedy', father?"

His father sniffed several times, and Gofreddo noted that a single tear now clung to the corner of his eye. This was not something too out of the ordinary since Gofreddo had often seen his father crying. Indeed, his father had often instilled on him the fact that crying was nothing for a man to be ashamed of; that, on the contrary, it showed a healthy emotional soul.

Now, though, it riled and confused Gofreddo.

Almost a sense of betrayal.

"What didn't you tell me, father?"

His father reached for a tissue, blew his nose, and then dabbed at his eyes. "Your *abuelito*, he was an astronaut, son—he was one of the men on board the Lunar One ..."

Gofreddo scowled at this. Of course, just like anyone else, he knew of the Lunar One Disaster—the tragedy which'd befallen the first mission to colonise the Moon. "I don't understand." He paused, stretched his mind back, to when he had visited the Moon with his father. "But we went to the memorial spot . . . we stood there, and we ..."

And then Gofreddo recalled his father's reaction at the memorial.

The tears.

He had thought it nothing out of the ordinary; that his father was merely expressing his sadness at the loss of such precious human life; at the loss of such fearless explorers.

Now, though, he saw that it had been more than that.

It had been more personal than that.

"I thought of telling you, when we were up in the Dome, but . . ."

Here his father trailed off as if he was lost in his thoughts.

"It never seemed the right time?" Gofreddo finished for him.

His father swallowed hard, and then nodded.

Gofreddo waited a long few moments, and then shook his head, turning his attention back to his father. "And why're you choosing to tell me this now? Why is this relevant to my plans on the Moon? To my project? Would you prefer I did not go through with it out of respect for *Abuelito*?

His father shook his head. "No," he said, "that's not it—not at all."

Gofreddo felt his chest become tight.

A heat flushed through his blood.

If there was something which was guaranteed to rile him, it was when his father kept secrets. When he deemed him unworthy to know some detail about the family business, or about the family history, because he simply 'wouldn't understand'.

"Your *abuelito*," his father continued, "he was buried on the Moon—he was among the first human beings to be put to rest when Lunar Two arrived with the second *successful* colonisation mission." His father's voice became too croaky for him to speak for several moments. He swallowed again—*hard*—getting himself back under control. "All I ask of you, Gofreddo, is that you bury your *abuelita* alongside him; that is her wish."

If Gofreddo had been feeling something approaching anger before, now he felt a freezing-cold wave pass over him. "*Abuelita* has passed away?"

His father shook his head. "No, son, but I fear it shall not be very long away."

Gofreddo held himself very still.

He could hear his heart beating thickly in his throat now.

In his eardrums.

"Will you come, father?" Gofreddo said. "Will you make the return journey with her?"

Again, his father shook his head. "No, son, I have already said goodbye to my father, and I do not wish to do so again. In any case, you are already there. You can take care of her—ensure that she is kept comforted in her final days." He cleared his throat, the tears now streaming freely down his cheeks. "It is for this reason that Wendy has gone away, with *Abuelita*. The two of them are travelling to the Launch Centre now. They shall be with you in the next few days."

It was overwhelming for Gofreddo.

He could feel himself welling up too.

But he forced himself to respond to his father. "We shall speak soon. And I will be sure to take good care of *Abuelita*. I shall take good care of her *for you.*"

And, with that, the screen went blank.

Gofreddo was left alone in the darkened room.

MANUAL RESEARCH ENGAGED

he Armstrong Archive grew up and around Alicia. Although it was tucked away near to the very fringes of the Celestial Stays Dome, it was arguably the most architecturally accomplished building on the lunar surface. Well, Alicia thought so, anyway.

The panels with which the building had been constructed were all transparent, so as to allow the sunlight, and the artificial, bright-white light through. As Alicia plodded up to the front desk, currently staffed by a droid, she couldn't help getting the feeling that the place was entirely made for her; that *she* was the only reason it existed.

For this precise moment now.

There were some guests arriving from Estonia later on and Alicia had been tasked with preparing some traditional Estonian cuisine for their visit. It was an important part of a Celestial Stays staff member's responsibilities to strive to make the service for the guests as bespoke as possible.

And so here she was.

She had put her request to the droid, and the droid had pointed her in the appropriate direction.

Although Alicia could just as easily have passed a request through the Link, via her earpiece, to fire her some Estonian recipes, she preferred the setting of the Armstrong Archive. It allowed her time and space to think without the daily distractions all around her. Whenever she put her mind to cooking a new recipe, she needed all the brain power she could get. She needed all her powers of concentration to make everything as delicious as she could manage.

All of the records held within the Armstrong Archive were paper: books or folders of collected information. Alicia recalled doing a school project on the importance of the Armstrong Archive, about how it acted as a physical store for human knowledge, if technology should fail mankind.

Or if mankind should annihilate itself.

Which one was most likely to come to pass, Alicia wouldn't like to guess.

In the end, following the codes written out on plastic cards, Alicia located the Estonian cultural section. She flipped through the records, searching for anything which might help her with the mission she'd assigned herself that day.

Several of the books, of course, were written in what Alicia took to be Estonian. Although she often prided herself on being a woman of the world, she had to admit that she was somewhat stumped by the words written out on the spines. Thankfully, though, she managed to come across a book with an English title; and with an exceptionally useful name:

Simple Estonian Recipes

She flipped through the pages looking at the pictures, as she always did with recipe books. She finally came across what looked to be an easy option which carried a large amount of scope for customisation and embellishment.

The name of the pudding was *karask*.

It looked almost like bread in the picture with a single dollop of vanilla ice cream in the process of melting on top of a single slice.

She glanced across the recipe and made a note, via the Link, of the ingredients she would need later on. That done, the information was automatically sent to her kitchen staff so that they could set about acquiring the ingredients . . . so that they could dig them out of storage, ready for her to work her magic.

She slipped the book back onto the shelf and then nearly jumped out of her skin to find herself nose to nose with someone.

She was so taken off-guard that it took her several seconds to bring her vision straight; to prevent the person standing before her from being just a single indistinct blur.

Strangely, the first feature which her eyes latched onto was the Mexican flag sewn onto the breast pocket of the man's royal-blue, Celestial Stays overalls.

Then she read the name:

M. CRUZ

Miguel Cruz.

The man who ran the Armstrong Archive.

Alicia flushed when she took in his close-cut hairline, and the tattoos which just about snuck out from beneath the upturned collar of his overalls. Although she'd been doing nothing wrong, she couldn't help but feel as if she'd been up to no good somehow.

"Find what you're looking for?" Miguel said, with a smile.

"Yes, I did, thanks," she replied.

Miguel nodded as if this was by-the-by.

From the way he was reaching out a hand to lean up against the book stack, it did seem as if his interest in whether or not she found what she was looking for was very much beside the point.

What *was* it with men and coming onto her these past few days?

Couldn't she skip out to the Archive anymore?

Even so, even despite her annoyance at this intrusion on her fact-finding mission, she couldn't help but note Miguel's muscular forearms; how he casually drummed his thick fingertips up against the metal casing of the book stack.

"Listen," Miguel said, breaking off eye contact and turning his eyes down to the toes of his boots, "Julius told me to come tell you something, okay?"

Alicia felt her heart drop.

If she never heard another *word* about Julius Denisov then it would be too soon. She knew that Julius and Miguel had a weekly poker game at the Stellar Tide—strictly big betting, and, from what she'd intuited, a *boys-only* club.

She couldn't think of many more boring things than sitting about a dimly lit, felt-clothed table for hours on end playing with colourful pieces of plastic and strips of laminated cardboard.

But, as a consequence, she had got to know Miguel.

Or, at least, she'd see him in Julius's company from time to time.

She supposed they were *friends*.

"Listen," Alicia said, making a move to pass Miguel, "I really don't have *time* for this."

She was glad that Miguel was gentleman enough not to impose his physicality on her. He didn't try to block her flight, as Julius would so often do whenever they had a fight; indeed as he had done when they'd faced off back in the kitchen of the Orbital Café.

Miguel did trail on her heels, though. "You should just know how chewed up he is with everything—how *bad* he feels about what happened to you . . . how he got you barred from your kitchen."

Alicia continued her journey toward the exit of the Archive. "He *didn't* get me barred from the kitchen—it was only for one day." This time she came to a halt and turned around; making a point of staring Miguel right back in the eye.

She knew how that simple gesture could unsettle men.

To Miguel's credit, he didn't look away.

"Anyway," she continued, "it was my own fault; I was the one who blew up . . . I was the one who *stormed* into his place of work and caused a fuss. I deserved punishment."

She resumed her route to the door of the Archive.

Miguel continued to follow in her footsteps. "Please, Alicia," he said. "Julius asked me if you would meet with him; if you'd just give him one chance. He said that if it doesn't work out this time then he'll promise to leave you alone forever."

A smile crept onto her lips.

She spun around, went nose-to-nose with Miguel. "Do you *really* think that one's going to work on me? Do I *look* like a total sucker?"

"No," Miguel replied, a touch dejectedly, taking a step backward.

"You can tell *Julius* that he can damn well go find another girl. *And* you can inform him that if we weren't stuck on the *Moon* together then I'd have no hesitation in attempting to get just as far away from him as I could possibly manage." She stopped, drew a profound breath and then stared Miguel in the eye. "Is that *clear*?"

Miguel held very still, and then gave a nod. "Yes," he said. "I'll tell Julius."

Alicia flashed her eyes at him. "All-righty, then, let's forget this conversation even happened."

As she made to move off, Miguel made another sound.

Eyes blazing, the same rage as that day when she'd stormed in on Julius, she turned on Miguel, ready to raise all kinds of fire and brimstone. *"What?"* she said. "What *the hell* is it?"

Miguel coloured slightly.

His eyes danced from one side to the other, and then he finally came out with it.

"I just thought you should know that someone's been following you—about the Archive."

"What?" Alicia said, her anger checked by this unexpected statement. "What're you talking about?"

Miguel jerked his thumb over his shoulder as if this explained everything.

When Alicia looked she saw, over at one of the book stacks, Kyra leafing through pages, apparently occupied in whatever it was she had come to the Archive to study.

Frowning, Alicia turned back to Miguel.

Then she cracked a grin.

"Yeah," Alicia said, "haven't you heard? The whole Celestial Stays administration thinks that I'm a psycho . . . they're keeping their eye on me everywhere—don't want me to break out and go crazy, do we? We don't want another episode like the one back at The Stellar Tide."

"No," Miguel said, backing away, and, for the first time in their conversation truly looking a touch flustered—*panicked* even. "We certainly don't."

With a severe smile, she turned away from Miguel and headed for the door.

It seemed almost as if she was shaking all over.

As if she might lose her balance and fall to the ground.

Why couldn't people just keep themselves to themselves?

"Alicia? Alicia?"

The voice called her from behind.

Feeling in a somewhat combative mood, she turned on her heel and stared off at the façade of the Armstrong Archive. For a second—for just a *second*—she thought that Miguel might be calling her back; that he might've been lining up just *one more shot* for his buddy Julius . . .

But it wasn't Miguel.

It was Kyra.

Alicia's personal 'spy'.

Although Alicia had the urge to turn away from Kyra, to leave her in the dust from her boots, she remained standing where she was. Despite knowing that she *should* hate Kyra—that she should hate the girl who'd been given the task of reporting back to senior management about Alicia's behaviour—she just couldn't bring herself to do it.

There was something about Kyra which seemed almost puppy-like; some quality she possessed which made her impossible to hate.

All the same, Alicia was hardly in the mood to jaw about this, that, or the other, after the unpleasant conversation she'd just had with Miguel.

"Are you okay, Alicia?" Kyra said, all wide-eyed and innocent.

Alicia had to grant Mackenzie one thing, she surely knew how to pick just the right spies. She knew how to pick the ones which would be impossible to take as a serious threat. "Fine," Alicia replied, stomping her way onward, toward the PEAR landing pad.

"Heading back to the café?" Kyra said.

"Uh-huh."

"You mind if we share a PEAR?"

Alicia shrugged. "Don't think there's anything I can do to stop you—don't want to give you something to write up to Mackenzie." She paused now, stared long and hard at Kyra. "Or maybe I *should* give you something to hand over to Mackenzie. Maybe that'll earn you some kudos, at the very least."

Alicia knew that she'd allowed her emotions to get the better of her once again, and she turned her back on Kyra, headed for the landing pad; all het up that she'd only succeeded in letting herself down.

The PEAR had hardly settled onto the landing pad when she felt Kyra's gentle touch on her arm. If it had been anyone else—just about *anyone* else on the face of the Moon—Alicia was convinced that she would've broken their arm . . . but since it was docile, harmless Kyra, she couldn't bring herself to cause her any kind of damage.

"Alicia?" Kyra said, a slight hop to her voice.

God, Alicia hoped she wasn't going to burst into tears.

That would be simply too much to bear.

Too much for her to have to *deal* with.

"I'd like to get to know you better," Kyra said. "So that we might be friends."

The PEAR's visor levered open on its arm.

From the slight *squeal* its hydraulics gave, Alicia judged that it could do with a few squirts of oil. But if she was so concerned about it, she could inform Maintenance later on. For the time being, she just clambered in over the side and took her seat.

Kyra got in beside her.

As the visor descended, Alicia felt Kyra's body warmth come to bear against her own. It was, all at once, intimate, awkward, uncomfortable, and . . . *reassuring.*

Alicia supposed that she was more and more confused these days.

The PEAR lifted off the landing pad, and it soon swept them over the lunar plains.

Alicia turned her attention upward, to the Earth as it hung in the sky above them.

"I heard you did a lot of travelling."

Alicia shifted Kyra a sidelong glance.

She waited a beat, and then said, "Who told you that?"

Kyra shrugged. "Just heard stories, that's all."

Alicia felt her stomach tighten into a knot.

That was the thing about living on the Moon.

Everybody seemed to know *everything.*

Gossip, like mould, thrived in a Petri dish like the Celestial Stays Dome.

"Yeah," Alicia replied, not seeing any point in hiding the truth. "That's right."

Kyra seemed to sense the tension hanging in the air. She allowed the conversation to settle for about a minute before asking her next question. "And what led you to *wanting* to travel?"

Alicia felt a slight smile line her lips. "You mean, what tipped the scales so badly that I completely lost it and ended up on the Moon?"

Kyra smiled back. "If you're crazy then it makes two of us."

"Thanks," Alicia replied, snorting a half-laugh.

"Go on, tell me why," Kyra said.

Alicia could see the Orbital Café growing up out of the lunar plains ahead. She knew that in a matter of minutes they would be back in the kitchen. That Alicia would be back in her element. That she would be able to forget about anything else and just focus her mind down into her hands, into *cookery*.

Alicia continued to stare ahead as she spoke. "I grew up on a farm out in the middle of nowhere." She slipped Kyra a glance. "Wood Dale, Illinois."

"The Prairie State," Kyra replied. "The Land of Lincoln."

Alicia blinked in disbelief. "Yeah," she said. "That's right."

Kyra smiled back. "I used to work in a call centre," she said. "Back in Delhi. Our clients, they were in the United States." She reached out and gestured at the PEAR's visor, as if pointing out some invisible feature. "On the walls there we would have all sorts of information about the areas where we received our customers." She looked back at Alicia. "The idea was to foster a *rapport* with the callers, so that we'd be more than just some anonymous *foreign-sounding* voice on the other end."

Here Kyra smiled wider, and then gave a brief peal of laughter.

It was endearing to Alicia; a real girlish, callow tone to it.

Kyra continued, "One time I remember almost having an argument with a customer. I do not recall where they were from, but we ended up speaking about Illinois. And this lady, this lady I was speaking to, she was *convinced* that the capital of Illinois was Chicago, and I kept telling her that, no, it was Springfield . . . but she would hear nothing at all about it." Kyra eyed Alicia closely. "Once I got off the phone, she remained convinced that the capital of Illinois was Chicago, and that was all there was to it." She took a deep breath as if she'd just completed some grand athletic feat. "That's the thing with people, don't you think, if you begin to argue with them they only become more determined—more *entrenched* in their own position."

Alicia also had the urge to tell Kyra that there was such a thing as native English speakers who didn't throw words like 'entrenched' around in usual conversations; and who didn't make the rote-learning of state capitals the priority it no doubt should have been in their lives.

"So," Kyra said, "I'm sorry for interrupting . . . *why* did you leave your farm? Why did you leave your family?"

The Orbital Café filled the entire landscape before the PEAR now.

Alicia studied its Alpine design. She felt as if she could already smell the sweet odours of baking. It wouldn't be long before she was back in her element.

Before she was back in her own personal *safe* place.

Here Alicia felt as if her mind was getting away from her again.

As if her strength was deserting her once more.

"Things changed," Alicia said.

"A death in the family?" Kyra said.

Alicia felt her stomach sink.

She turned full onto Kyra. "Yes," she said. "How did you know?"

Kyra swallowed hard and then inspected the backs of her hands, which, Alicia noted, had been extremely well cared for; maintained nicely moisturised. Finally, she glanced up, caught Alicia's eye. "Just a guess."

The PEAR drew into the landing pad, and slowed right down.

Alicia waited until the PEAR had come to a complete halt and the visor was sliding back, letting them free from the capsule, before she continued.

"It was my grandmother," Alicia said. "We were close—*really* close."

It was completely silent on the landing pad.

Just Alicia and Kyra.

Nobody else close by.

It felt intimate.

Almost as if they were alone on an abandoned lunar colony.

"She taught me everything," Alicia said, with a sigh. "She was the one who ignited my passion for cooking. She's the reason that I'm here at all . . . that I'm on the *Moon*."

Kyra's eyes widened in understanding.

Her lips were pert, and pretty, and waiting to empathise.

"When she got ill"—here Alicia felt her voice begin to wobble, as it always did whenever she found herself speaking about her grandmother—"I took care of her; I was the one who cooked her meals, who brought her medicines." Alicia gave a shake of her head. "And then . . . and then, one day . . . I just couldn't take it any longer; seeing how she was—the *state* she was in . . . how I was only . . . only . . ."

Now Alicia felt Kyra take hold of her hand.

Give it a squeeze.

Alicia swallowed hard. Then she gathered herself together. "It felt that I was only waiting for her to die, and I couldn't take it . . . not anymore . . . I . . . I don't know . . . somehow seeing her in that bed, in our family home, it was like I was looking into the future; seeing a part of myself—*myself*—finishing up just where I'd started." Tears in her eyes now, she turned on Kyra. "I'm sorry," she said, near to hysterical laughter, "that makes *no* sense."

Kyra only squeezed her hand more tightly still. "No," she replied. "It makes *perfect* sense; believe me, I know too what it is to lose somebody close . . . to lose somebody who you always thought would be there."

Alicia took a succession of deep breaths, trying to get her emotions under some kind of control; trying to get her mind prepared for the shift that needed to be put in.

She had the *karask* to prepare for the esteemed Estonian guests. That would take her mind off the past.

At least for a while.

"All right," Alicia said, eyeing Kyra closely. "I think we should get to work—don't you think?"

Kyra nodded back at her, gave her hand a final squeeze, and then the two of them clambered up and out of the PEAR.

13

LAUNCH PREPARATIONS

endy Flowme could feel her heart racing.

Although she had gone through more rotations than she wanted to think about beneath the Celestial Stays Dome, the whole process of taking off into space still overwhelmed her somewhat. She supposed that it was an intrinsic sense of wonder. And, to be honest, she wouldn't like to live to see the day when it eventually deserted her.

'Wonder', she had always thought, separated mankind from the animals.

This was a somewhat different task from that which she was used to, though.

Escorting her boyfriend's mother on a one-way trip to the Moon.

It felt strange to think that Costantino Zito was her *boyfriend*, although things had certainly moved beyond the mind-blowing, simian sex sessions into something more serious. She knew that it was quite another step for Costantino to trust his own mother to her. And Wendy had no intention of letting him down.

If there was one thing which she had proved to herself and others throughout her life, it was that she was reliable; that she could be relied upon come what may.

She turned in her seat, to take in Costantino's mother, Paula, now.

As with everyone else loaded into the space elevator, she was dressed in the thermal suit with a helmet brought down over her head. Although Wendy could only make out a small portion of her wrinkled, pallid flesh through the visor of the helmet, she could tell that she was smiling.

Wendy turned away from Paula, and looked to the front preparing for the launch.

It truly blew her mind at how quickly things had moved. That once Costantino had got his heart set on the idea—of his mother breathing her last on the Moon—he wouldn't be shifted. He had gone to work on all the relevant authorities, speaking with all kinds of administrative staff, attempting to get the idea made reality.

And, as with pretty much everything in his entire life until this point, he had succeeded.

Paula would pass away on the Moon.

Be buried beside her husband who had perished in the Lunar One Disaster.

Just to think about it brought a tear to Wendy's eye.

She had always held a special place in her heart for explorers . . . and especially those who took to exploring space.

A message sounded through Wendy's earpiece, and she closed her eyes.

Soon she would be back.
Back on the Moon.

14

LEISURELY RENDEZVOUS

here was a strong scent of baking barley bread.

The *karask*. The surprise she was baking especially for the Estonian visitors.

It would be ready soon enough.

Alicia reached up and wiped the thin layer of perspiration which'd seeped out of her forehead. And she took a well-earned breath, feeling as if she was refreshing her muscles and frayed nerves.

Although she would never in a hundred years have thought it possible, when she reached the end of her shift at the Orbital Café, she actually felt *less* stressed than when she had started.

Usually after a whole day's worth of supervising her staff— what she had come to see as 'damage limitation'—she would feel as if she was ready to go to sleep for a month, only to have to get up the next day and do it all over again. This time, though—*today*— she had laughed her way through all the minor problems which'd cropped up; even the part when Drake had unceremoniously tossed out the greater part of the ingredients for the *karask*.

Instead of shouting at him, as was her go-to response, she had kept her wits about her. She had merely told him, in a calm, clear voice, to go and fetch another batch of ingredients out of storage.

Her staff had noted her more-cheerful-than-normal mood, and she had noticed them smiling back at her. She couldn't remember the last time she had caught her staff smiling and she knew that only one person could be held responsible for the lightening of tensions within the Orbital Café kitchens. Kyra.

It was the combination of having unburdened herself on the ride over from the Armstrong Archive, along with the fact that she could now count on another friend.

What was it people said about it being impossible to have too many friends?

Was there any truth in it?

She knew what her grandmother would've told her; that, in real life, you couldn't count on anybody or anything . . . it was all down to you. To the individual.

And Alicia considered that she had only gone on to prove *that* particular hypothesis . . .

She ducked down at the oven, dustpan and brush in her hands. She glanced back over her shoulder to her kitchen staff.

Millat. Stéphanie. And Drake.

All of them smiling from ear to ear as they went about their dedicated duties.

She felt the good will near enough *flushing* through her.

"It's okay," she said. "You guys are dismissed—go and have yourselves a good evening; there's another hard day's work coming up tomorrow."

Despite the relaxed atmosphere which'd surrounded the whole

day in the kitchen, Alicia noted their hesitancy. They couldn't quite believe this change in their boss. But Alicia was determined that they would see that she *had* changed.

"Go on," she said, with a grin this time.

After exchanging glances between themselves, all three of her kitchen staff removed their aprons and paper hats, hanging them up on the hook on their way out of the door.

Soon enough it left Alicia and Kyra alone.

Alicia turned her attention to Kyra. "I meant you too," she said, sweeping up a piece of pastry which'd somehow sprung free of the oven.

As Alicia stooped down low, to get at some more of the muck which'd accumulated beneath the oven, she was aware of Kyra's retreating footsteps. She noted how she hesitated before going out through the door.

"Thanks," Kyra said.

"Don't mention it," Alicia replied. "I guess we've all earned ourselves a break after the shift we put in today."

"No, I didn't mean to thank you for *that.*"

Alicia glanced up, still smiling. "For what, then?" she replied.

"For taking me in," Kyra said. "For making me feel like your friend."

A warmth glowed deep in Alicia's gut. "We *are* friends, aren't we?"

Kyra shrugged, grinning. "I suppose."

She lingered another few moments in the doorway, before wishing Alicia a good night and heading off out.

Alicia waited until she heard the side door to the Orbital Café swing shut before allowing herself a profound sigh. The grin lessened its hold on her face. She brushed up some more. Her smile finally gave way to a neutral pout. And then, for no reason she could quite determine, she realised that she was crying.

Suddenly devoid of strength, she allowed the dustpan and brush to drop from her hands.

They fell at her feet with a clatter.

She remained stooped, glad to know that she was hidden behind the preparation counters; that even if there'd been anybody else with her there, in the café, nobody would have been able to see her cry.

Although today had been peaceful, and Alicia felt physically invigorated, she had to admit that, emotionally, she was feeling somewhat spent.

To think about the conversation she'd shared with Kyra.

About her grandmother.

She hadn't shared that information with *anyone*.

How she hadn't been able to be with her grandmother when she had most needed it.

How she had run away.

A *coward*.

It was then that Alicia heard the door to the Orbital Café swinging open again.

Her whole body went rigid.

She sucked in a breath.

Wondered if it might be Kyra.

Although the two of them had shared a tender moment earlier that day, it seemed somehow inappropriate that they should go through that same rigmarole all over again. Despite feeling glad that she had had the chance to unburden herself, Alicia doubted that it marked a complete change of her personality.

She wasn't willing to let herself go.

Not quite yet.

It was as she straightened up, smoothing the wrinkles out of the apron she still wore over her overalls that a far worse realisation dawned over her. She studied the footsteps. Their rhythm. Their *weight*. And she knew that it couldn't possibly be Kyra.

The steps were too heavy.

She could hear throaty, *manly* breaths.

The truth hit her like a damp rag.

Julius. Julius *fucking* Denisov.

It couldn't be . . . could it?

Was he going to ignore Alicia's response to his request for a 'second chance'?

That she had no intention of falling into another trap?

Alicia glanced about the kitchen, searching for some sort of weapon. Just in case.

Finally, she settled on a large, recently sharpened knife.

A knife which Stéphanie had been using earlier to chop hazelnuts.

As Alicia crouched down, behind one of the preparation counters, she could still smell the earthy scent of hazelnut clinging to the blade. There was something about that particular aroma which sent her mind spinning back to Earth . . . all over again.

She pushed reminiscence away.

She pushed *memory* away.

And she concentrated on the present.

Waited for Julius . . .

As his footsteps became louder still, she pressed her back up against the counter.

Bided her time.

Surprise would be her main strength here.

Perhaps it would be her *sole* advantage.

The footsteps came to a halt.

She listened to the thick, masculine breathing.

Could she sense a note of panic there?

Might Julius do something he might regret?

... It'd been a good idea to arm herself.

He took another couple of steps into the kitchen.

Alicia tightened her grip about the handle of the knife.

The hazelnuts got stronger in her nostrils.

Just like being back home.

Back on the farm.

She could almost *breathe* that fresh air now.

... He stood over her.

Just to the side of her.

This was her chance.

This *was* her chance!

With a single, clean motion, she leaped up.

She held the knife level with her chest.

The blade pointed to the floor.

Ready to bring it *stabbing* down.

He faced away from her.

She had the view of his shoulders.

When she spoke, her voice was surprisingly firm.

Surprisingly *sure*.

"If you move, I'll *kill* you."

Despite this threat, he turned around.

And—in retrospect—it was probably a good thing too.

Because she saw that it wasn't Julius at all.

It was Gofreddo.

"Goodness," Gofreddo said, turning around to face her, his eyes instantly locking onto the knife which Alicia held tight in her fist, ready to stab him with.

He held his hands up, more a sort of knee-jerk reaction than any kind of serious surrender. He was still clearly bemused by the turn of events.

And Alicia didn't blame him.

She must look like a total loon right now.

She *felt* like a total loon herself.

. . . Yet she'd been so sure that it'd been Julius.

She'd had to be careful.

Had to think of her own safety *first*.

As if this intense situation required an intense reaction, Alicia released the knife and it tumbled down through the air, clattering on the floor.

Gofreddo continued to hold his hands up.

"Sorry," Alicia said, "I thought you were someone else."

Gofreddo allowed his hands to drop. He glanced down at the knife, now lying at their feet, and reflecting the bright, even lighting of the kitchen. "Clearly." He looked back up at Alicia, then smiled. "The question, I suppose, is just *who*?"

Perhaps still working on some kind of adrenalin high from the whole situation, Alicia replied with a snap to her voice. "No one important—just someone who keeps hanging around."

Gofreddo smiled more broadly still. "Remind me never to get into your bad books, eh?"

"It's okay," Alicia replied. "Really—I'm not a violent person."

Gofreddo sniffed a laugh. "That's a pity," he said. "I've always had something of a like for those with red-blooded passion."

Alicia rolled her eyes, again without thinking it through clearly. "That's what men always *think* they want until they end up being on the other end." Her mouth twisted at one corner. "Then they always want to surrender or escape."

The knife now apparently forgotten for the time being, Gofreddo took a step toward her. His blond hair, as always, stuck up in tufts, and his sky-blue eyes had a quick, swift quality to them. She supposed that this was a kind of reflection of his smarts; those smarts which he shared with his father. Those smarts which'd gone on to conquer the world.

And which might now conquer the Moon too.

Let alone Alicia's heart.

As Gofreddo stepped into her, she felt his warm breath up against her skin. She caught a whiff of the day-old cologne he wore, mixed in with that musky smell of hard work.

He reached out and brushed the hair from the side of her face with his pleasantly moisturised hands. She couldn't help noticing —with a touch of surprise—that his palms were slightly calloused; just like her own had been back when she'd been a girl on the farm.

Perhaps the rich didn't live as her family had always believed.

Maybe they didn't have legions of workers to do whatever they said for minimal pay.

But that all seemed so by-the-by . . .

He leaned in and pressed his lips up against hers.

His mouth was pleasantly soft.

He nibbled at her lower lip playfully; awaiting her response.

And she *responded*.

Just as she felt as if she was reaching the point when she would melt completely, he arched his shoulders back. He took her in with his wide, blue eyes as if he could never widen them far enough to fully appreciate her.

Was this how men were supposed to treat women?

Was this what her grandmother had always told her about how men should put their women up on a pedestal?

"Alicia," he said, "I have a question for you."

"Okay."

Gofreddo breathed in deeply. His eyes skipped over hers, and then he reached out and ran his fingers through her hair again. "What would you think if I decided to stay here—if I decided to spend more time up on the Moon?"

Although she felt as if her stomach sank clean through the floor, and a prickling sensation skittered clear across her skin, she managed to keep her expression neutral.

Businesslike almost.

"Why," she replied. "I'm sure I'd like it just fine."

She even threw in a smile for good measure.

Gofreddo smiled back at her, albeit briefly.

Now that she took him in for the first time properly, she couldn't help but notice those black rings which clung to the bottoms of his eyes. He seemed to have that same slightly pallid tone to his complexion as that day when they had first kissed in the Crescent Gardens.

"What's wrong?" she said. "What's on your mind?"

Gofreddo glanced back at her, again attempting a smile, but having it slip clean off his lips before it really got going. "It's just a little bit of everything," he said. "Personal. *Business.*" He breathed a husky sigh. "Just my *life*, that's all . . . it's all a bit of a . . . uh . . . *mindfuck.*"

Alicia blinked a couple of times at the expression.

To begin with she'd thought that he'd been searching for the right word, and, well—if he had—then he'd surely found it.

"In what way?" Alicia said, now feeling a touch light-headed and reaching back for the edge of the counter to gain some much-needed stability.

"Oh, you know," he said, "it's difficult, like I said, for me to open up to anybody; for me to *trust* anybody." Here he caught her eye and gave her a slack-mouthed grin."

Although Alicia did her best to hide the sting of this comment, she realised that she must've shown off at least a little pain in her quick response. "You mean it's difficult to trust me?"

"I . . . no," he replied. "It's just that—"

"You've been stung before?" Alicia replied, doing her best to shove her own ego to one side for the time being.

"Yes," he said, again flashing her an apologetic smile. When he sighed, his shoulders slackened and his whole body seemed to deflate. "It's nothing personal, but it will just take time. I need to *feel* ready in someone else's company." He looked at Alicia again. "Do you understand what I mean?"

Despite feeling somewhat subdued by this whole conversation, when she'd been flying so high during that kiss, Alicia managed a nod by way of reply. "Yes," she said. "I understand." She drew a deep breath of her own. "You just need time. Time to *trust* me, that's all . . . and you're willing to *give* it time."

Gofreddo smiled widely. "Thank you," he said. "It means so much to me; you don't know what it means to find someone like you; someone who makes me feel like . . . like . . ." He flushed slightly, the blush bringing some much-needed colour to his pale skin. "Like I *do*," he finally got out.

A profound silence fell on the kitchen and Alicia felt her heart bouncing up to her throat.

Her body craved another kiss.

One equally as passionate as the one before.

But now the mood had shifted.

Everything had changed.

Right when she believed Gofreddo was preparing to leave—that he was going to make some comment to excuse himself—he surprised her.

He leaned into her.

"Listen, Alicia, I trust you," he said. "I want you to know that." He reached down for her hand, entwined his fingers with hers. "And I wish to prove it to you."

Alicia knew that it was her turn to be quiet.

To allow Gofreddo to speak.

But she couldn't help herself.

She liked concrete answers too much.

She liked to know where she *stood* too much.

"How?" she said.

15

APPROPRIATE CONNECTIONS

*G*ofreddo's *stomach* felt as if it wouldn't settle itself down ever again. As he waited within Entry Clearance for Wendy Flowme, and his *abuelita*, to appear, he realised he was still trying to get his head around all that had gone on over the past few days; the past few weeks. It seemed as though everything had happened so quickly. A new project. A new *love*. And he had learned something of his family history.

Something which had always been kept from him.

If he had learned one thing through his life of being Costantino Zito's son, it was how to cope with pressure. How to keep himself together when it seemed as if the world might be ready to come tumbling down about his ears.

First, he reached down and pinched the veins at his wrist with his index finger and thumb. He felt his pulse gently throbbing beneath his fingertips; his heart giving a gentle kick as it acknowledged the sensation.

This was a trick his grandmother herself had taught him.

Often, while travelling around near their farm, they would drive along curving, hilly roads. Gofreddo would often feel himself growing nauseous as the journey went on. He must have been about five or six years old when it seemed that on just about every single trip he took with his father in a car, he would finish the journey throwing up.

His father was never angry, of course, but Gofreddo could always detect the subtle disappointment in his voice, as if he was struggling to hold back his frustration.

Perhaps one of the only times he had ever felt his father suggest any kind of volatile, out-of-control emotion.

But once Gofreddo's grandmother had taught him this trick of pinching his wrist, he had utilised it every journey since. And he had never got sick again.

As per arrangements, Gofreddo's grandmother was brought along in a motorised wheelchair; one of those sleek, transparent designs which Gofreddo's father had got on prototype from one of his Japanese acquaintances. Gofreddo could recall overhearing the man in the hallway of their home waxing lyrical in loud, truncated English about the various features of the wheelchair. And he had to admit that the wheelchair's ability to travel over just about any terrain *was* a valuable feature for their particular situation back on the farm. Just as it was now, here, on the Moon.

With Wendy's help, Gofreddo lifted his grandmother's wheelchair into the PEAR which arrived outside of Entry Clearance. After Gofreddo had got in beside his grandmother—who was sleeping soundly—Wendy waited to take the next PEAR which would arrive on the landing pad.

They headed directly to the Lunar Grand, and were helped by the hotel staff up to the Blue Moon Suite, which'd been specially selected by Gofreddo's father as the perfect venue for Paula Zito to spend her last days. Even though Gofreddo was close to his grandmother—and able to see her infirm state for himself—he couldn't bring himself to *quite* believe that she was nearing the end of her life. She had always been there. *Always* present.

But, he supposed, everything had to go away in the end.

Everyone had to.

The suite itself was wonderful.

Gofreddo had, of course, taken a brief tour of the suite. But he hadn't been quite in the right mind to savour each of the details: to look over the furnishings and decoration with quite the concentration it surely deserved. But, as he wheeled his grandmother over to the window which looked out over the lunar plains, he did so now.

The whole room was varying degrees of blue. The wallpaper itself was currently displaying a calming, powder-blue colour. The carpets were an even lighter shade of blue; almost the grey of the lunar surface itself, really. Finally, the furnishings—the sofas, chairs and picture frames—were all the royal-blue of Celestial Stays.

Gofreddo turned his attention to the pictures.

All of them, in one way, or another, were depictions of the Moon with a bluish hue.

Just from looking, he could tell that some of them had been completed using pastels, while others were from using chalk. There were a couple of watercolours, too.

He glanced over to his grandmother, saw that she was still sleeping, and knew that, if she'd been awake, she wouldn't have been able to have imagined a more beautiful room if she'd tried. That had been his intention. That had been his father's intention.

Why shouldn't his grandmother's final bedroom not be a beautiful one?

"You're sure this is okay?"

Gofreddo turned his attention to the doorway.

Picked out Wendy standing there, still in her grey-white flight suit; the same one which his grandmother wore. Although Entry Clearance usually dealt with matters such as wardrobe—the compulsory change into the appropriately coloured overalls—this protocol had been overlooked on this occasion. It had been decided, by his father, and whoever it involved back down on Earth, that Gofreddo's grandmother's arrival to the Moon should be kept as under wraps as possible . . . and not just because of the scandal it might whip up merely by the connection to someone as famous as Costantino Zito. No, there was still something of a lack of consensus about whether or not human beings should be permitted burial on the Moon. Lunar One, make no mistake, had been an exception. The matter had been fiercely debated, down on Earth, about what should be done in the event of a death up on the Moon. For the time being, regulation stated that the body should be flown back to Earth.

Although Gofreddo was obviously affected by his own personal bias, he couldn't help wondering if there couldn't be exceptions made to the rule.

Surely if an elderly lady's dying wish was to be laid to rest beside the man she had loved throughout life every effort should be made to respect that?

Since Gofreddo didn't reply, Wendy added, "You don't think that this is too blue? It's not too *depressing*?"

Although Gofreddo was certain that others might've been taken off-guard by Wendy's direct manner of speaking, he found her style refreshing. He smiled in reply, and said, "No, it's perfect."

"Good," Wendy said, smiling back, then jerking her thumb over her shoulder. "I'll go and check out what the culinary options are, okay?"

"All right," Gofreddo replied.

Wendy disappeared off down the corridor.

Gofreddo turned his attention back to his grandmother, and he was surprised to see that she was not only awake, but that she was staring at him, smiling.

"*Nieto*," she said, her voice fragile.

It put Gofreddo in mind of the bird's nests which he would see on the farm back home. The ones which would precariously balance between the tree branches, only to be brought down in the first harsh storm of winter.

He crouched down at his grandmother's side. He took her delicate hand which she held out to him. He felt her leathery skin, and her impossibly light bones. And he sensed her give him a slight squeeze. "*Abuelita*," he said.

"You are so good," she said, her voice faltering a little, "so good to indulge your grandmother like this, one last time. To give her something for all eternity."

Gofreddo's heart clenched.

He sensed his pulse beating hard in his temples.

When he felt a knot form in his throat, he swallowed it down.

"It was all we could do," he said. "All that me and *papá* could do."

"*Gracias.*"

Here it seemed that his grandmother became more frail; perhaps the arduous journey from Earth was finally having an effect on her. With the intention of giving his grandmother a well-deserved rest, Gofreddo slunk his way toward the door of the suite.

Only to hear her voice calling him back.

"Gofreddo? . . . Gofreddo?"

"*Abuelita?*"

Her neck was tilted to one side as she sat in her wheelchair. There was a slight smile lining her lips. "I am sorry for never telling you what happened to your *abuelito*, you have to understand that it was painful for me . . . that to know . . . to know . . ."

Here Gofreddo noticed a single, silvery tear sneak free from the corner of her eye.

His heart thumped hard.

But he stayed where he was, still standing in the middle of the room.

Gofreddo raised a smile.

His whole body chilled for a moment, and then warmed.

"I understand," he replied. "And I'll be back soon. Get some sleep, *Abuelita.*"

And, smiling in response, his grandmother closed her eyes and drifted away from him again.

16

DIFFERING OBJECTIVES

lthough Alicia was constantly chiding herself not to do it, she couldn't help it today.

She leaned against the wall in the customer area of the Orbital Café and watched on as the Estonian visitors all tried the warm *karask* she had poured so much time and effort into lovingly preparing. In the end, she had gone with her gut feeling, and arranged for each slice to be served with a scoop of vanilla ice cream.

There were five people in the group in all; what she took to be a man and wife, with their two children. A grandfather completed the group.

As she always did whenever she considered some aspect of the Orbital Café, she attempted to put herself in the customers' shoes; to see things from their perspective. And she was *quite sure* that it would be very low on her list of requirements to have a member of staff constantly staring at her while she was attempting to enjoy some supposedly delicious morsel or other.

And yet, she kept telling herself that it was for the benefit of experience.

That she could gather data from each customer's reaction; that she could deduce from a slight wince that the ice cream might've been served a touch too chilled, or learn from a spate of prolonged chewing that she could've overdone the base. Even though she doubted that she would be getting Shuttle loads of Estonians from now on, she would certainly make sure to add the *karask* to her inventory of baked goods that could be rustled up.

If there was one thing which kept her from ever being bored with cooking, it was the knowledge that, all the time, there were dishes just down there—*on planet Earth*—waiting to be discovered; still being *invented*.

Just as she'd been working on some culinary inventions of her own ...

She had to admit that it wasn't without a touch of ego that she'd started to believe she might have a key role in the development of lunar cuisine.

Although it seemed almost like a *silly* thing to be remembered for, it did seem like it *could* be something that she'd be remembered for. Since she'd dedicated so much of her life to baking, why not make it her legacy?

As Alicia made mental notes to herself according to her customers' reactions, she couldn't help but turn her thoughts back to what Gofreddo had told her; what he had *confided* in her. She had to admit that the information he'd dumped on her had had a sort of disorientating effect. She had felt dizzied by it all ... and so there was no telling how Gofreddo himself must've felt.

There was, of course, principally, the news that his grandmother was coming up to the Celestial Stays Dome as a visitor. But that was really just the start of it. He had gone on to relay to her about how they had decided—Gofreddo, his father, and his grandmother herself—that she would pass her final days here, on the Moon.

All the doctors said she had weeks to live.

If not *days*.

Alicia wasn't all that aware of current legislation concerning human burial on the Moon, although she had always been under the assumption that it was prohibited. When she had put this to Gofreddo, he had given her the glimmer of a smile and explained that there were 'extenuating circumstances'. That Gofreddo's grandfather had been on Lunar One.

That he had *perished* on Lunar One.

Of course Alicia had at first been almost unable to believe it. Just like every other schoolchild on the face of planet Earth, she had learned all about the Lunar One tragedy; the first mission intended to colonise the Moon. Their science teacher had gone through the mechanics of the mission's failure, starting with catastrophic take-off which apparently doomed any hope of landing. But the hope had remained, although to no end, because it had finished up with the heart-breaking finale, as the Shuttle failed to touch down smoothly on the lunar surface; crashing and bundling into a thousand different pieces. She supposed that they might've studied the crew roster at some point during her education, but she had no reason to take note of the many hundreds of names all listed out there. Among them there had been Costantino Zito Senior; Gofreddo's grandfather.

It had been a show of trust in Alicia that Gofreddo had confided such a personal matter in her. And Alicia had hardly been able to hide her own feelings; feelings about how she had lost her own grandmother, and in the way she'd believed herself to be neglectful..

As of yet, Gofreddo hadn't asked that she play any part in his grandmother's visit to the Celestial Stays Dome, and Alicia wouldn't presume anything.

She knew how big of a step it had been for Gofreddo to simply confide such a private detail in her. And she was determined to repay that trust.

Alicia lingered another moment looking over the Estonian guests, and she allowed herself a moment's glee at what she believed to be their overwhelming positive reaction to her *karask*. She straightened herself up, pulling herself away from the wall; her lower back having gone numb from the way she'd been leaning.

She returned to the kitchen, to find her staff in different poses; all of them performing different jobs which were required:

Chopping. Washing up. Tending to the oven.

And, in Kyra's case, kneading a mixture in a bowl, preparing to put in some gingerbread men to bake for the following day.

Kyra was the first to glance up and notice Alicia there. She smiled warmly. "I take it that the *karask* went well. I haven't heard any retching or sirens."

"What can I say?" Alicia replied, crossing her arms over her chest. "I pride myself on maintaining a kitchen which produces—day after day—edible foodstuffs."

Kyra turned her attention back downward, to the mixing she was doing. "Haven't you got a hot date lined up tonight? You do realise it's Friday, don't you?"

Alicia felt her chest tighten.

She *hadn't* realised it was Friday at all.

And to be quite honest Friday was usually much the same as Monday, Tuesday, Wednesday . . . or Saturday or Sunday, for that matter.

As for a 'hot date', Alicia was certain that Gofreddo had other things on his mind with his grandmother having just arrived.

"Go on," Kyra said, looking up from her work on the ginger-bread mixture.

" 'Go on' what?" Alicia replied.

"You let us out early the other day, now it's our turn to make it up for you." She gave the gingerbread dough a good few squeezes as if she was grinding home her point. "Have some fun. Let your hair down. We promise not to reduce the whole café to rubble, all right?"

Alicia felt stuck for several long moments; not quite able to let go.

She might not have a 'hot date' lined up, but she could certainly think of some ways to spend a lonely Friday night . . . and none of them involved getting down on her hands and knees to sweep up the kitchen floor of the Orbital Café.

Decided now, she turned and looked over her staff. "All righty," she said. "I'll take you up on that offer—I could do with some personal TLC."

"Go on," Kyra said, and then, looking up. "*Get* won't you?"

With a smile, Alicia slipped out of the kitchen, and caught a PEAR to the Basements.

Alicia had her heart set on a swim followed by a Jacuzzi, sauna and hot shower, but she found her plans were rudely shattered before she'd even begun. Her earpiece informed her that she had a message waiting from a certain Gofreddo Zito.

And, even after all that talk about 'patience' and 'subtlety', and whatever else, with Louise, she didn't seem able to control her body's will.

He told her to meet him at Entry Clearance in half an hour.

Although it hardly gave Alicia enough time to smudge on some makeup, she found herself accepting the offer. She really did suppose that this boy had somehow managed to get to her; had somehow managed to make her *smitten*.

On her way to Entry Clearance, travelling in the PEAR, she couldn't help but think of her romantic past; about all of those lovers who had come and gone, and how—no matter how long they lasted—they had never really become anything more than that.

Just lovers . . . to be discarded on a whim.

But Gofreddo was different.

And although she couldn't explain it, she could *feel* it.

She was surprised to find Gofreddo standing alone outside Entry Clearance.

Like her, he had changed out of his royal-blue Celestial Stays overalls.

Now he wore a simple, well-cut leather jacket over a pair of battered blue jeans.

Alicia had finally settled on a striped mauve-and-black dress which an ex-*lover* had once told her made her look like a witch. Although there was a multitude of ways that she might've taken that comment, she had decided to take it to mean a *sexy* witch.

She'd finished up the look with a pair of knee-high leather boots.

"Good evening," Gofreddo said, with a smile, and leaned into her.

He placed a gentle, *sweet* kiss on her lips.

One of those kisses which—if it had been from a former lover —would've only frustrated her.

But, coming from Gofreddo, it was delicious . . . an *appetiser*.

"Are you ready?" he said, pulling away.

"Ready for what?"

"For a trip."

Alicia frowned. "Where're we going?"

But Gofreddo only tapped the side of his nose by way of reply.

He reached down to take hold of her hand. He squeezed it gently but firmly, and he guided her along the side of the Entry Clearance building. She could already tell that they were headed for the Shuttle Pool. As they continued on their way, Alicia had the urge to ask after his grandmother; to ask whether she had arrived safely, and, perhaps, to enquire as to where she was right then.

But somehow it didn't seem appropriate.

She decided that she should just go with the flow.

Now that Gofreddo had trusted in her, it was time for her to return that trust.

To *trust* when he felt the time was right to share personal details of his life with her.

They cleared the security droids at the entrance of the Shuttle Pool—something which Alicia was certain required a certain *know-how* . . . no doubt Gofreddo had cribbed this knowledge from one of the other Shuttle pilots. Most likely Patrick Fourie.

It was a sight which she'd never seen within the Shuttle Hanger.

The dozen or so Shuttles were all lined up in an even row.

All of them with their noses pointing to the glass doors which led out to the lunar plains.

Just to stand up on the platform which was located above them, and to stare out across the lunar plains beyond the windows, was overwhelming.

All so barren.

All so empty.

So *alone.*

"I got special permission," Gofreddo said, beginning to explain. "For tomorrow morning; to bring my grandmother out to the Lunar One memorial site."

It seemed as if Alicia should say something in response.

But she could think of nothing appropriate.

Gofreddo continued, "I have clearance for the Shuttle Pool." He shrugged. "Though I guess they didn't mean for me to use it until tomorrow."

Alicia stepped past this breach in protocol.

Something which she didn't find too tough.

She was certain that she had broken more than her share of Celestial Stays's employee rules throughout the duration of her contract.

She turned away from the Shuttles. "What've you got in mind to do, then?" she said.

"Well," Gofreddo said, taking a step toward her; so that she could feel his warm breath against her face, "I thought we could take a private trip of our own."

Alicia arched an eyebrow. "And I suppose you've already drawn up the flight map—got it checked over and approved by Celestial Stays administration."

"Absolutely not."

For a long second or so, Gofreddo remained with his face uncomfortably close to hers.

Finally, right when she was certain he was going to lay a kiss on her lips, he pulled away.

"Come on," he said. "Time's a-wastin'."

Alicia was pleasantly surprised to find that the aerobatics were lacking on their 'special' trip.

Perhaps Gofreddo was just as attentive—just as *responsive*—to his clientele's feedback as Alicia herself was . . . always working out how best to tailor the service to the client; to *improve* the client's experience.

It was almost as if she lived by the contract she'd signed.

Alicia didn't press Gofreddo about details concerning their journey, although she couldn't help noticing they were making a beeline for the Lunar One crash site. As they closed in on the site itself, Gofreddo, again spontaneously, began to explain.

"This shall be the first time I have seen the Lunar One Monument since I learned that my grandfather was among the ones to perish in the tragedy."

Alicia had no idea what she should say.

And before she had fully thought through the implications of what Gofreddo had just told her, she found herself replying, "Why did you decide to bring *me*?"

Gofreddo went very quiet.

They travelled on across the lunar plains.

Neither one of them speaking.

Alicia was certain Gofreddo had forgotten she'd asked a question at all.

It was only when Alicia spotted the Lunar One Monument peeping out over the horizon—a carved stone statue of the Shuttle occupying the location of the crash—that Gofreddo picked up where he had left off. "I wanted to see it for myself—before I return tomorrow morning with my grandmother. Only . . ." his words tumbled away as he carefully steered the Shuttle onward ". . . I didn't want to come here alone."

17

EMOTIONAL INTERCHANGE

*A*s *the Shuttle settled down* on the lunar surface, Alicia felt her heart beat up into her throat. She sat still in the chair beside the captain's while Gofreddo stared out at the Lunar One Monument. She was aware of every single breath, of each one of her movements. She dedicated all her energy into not invading Gofreddo's personal moment with his grandfather.

Although it was probably no more than ten minutes, it felt as if they rested there for hours on end. Alicia's whole body had turned rigid once they'd been stationary for such a long time. Despite having been out on various Shuttle trips in the past, she'd never really had the chance to acknowledge just how remote it felt to be so far from the Celestial Stays Dome . . . with nothing in sight, save for the Lunar One Monument, she could quite easily allow her imagination to run wild; to believe that she and Gofreddo were the only ones on the Moon.

"Okay," Gofreddo said, turning away from the monument.

He remained side on, so that Alicia could only make out his

face in profile. The backdrop of stars served as a mystical reminder of just where they were. It might just as easily have been a movie set.

She studied him for any sign of tears, any outward emotion, but he somehow managed to set his features to an entirely neutral expression. As if they might've been just about anywhere at all; as if he wasn't mere metres away from his grandfather's grave.

Without another word, Gofreddo engaged the Shuttle's thrusters, boosting them back up off the lunar surface. They'd been flying for about two minutes when Alicia thought that she should raise the issue she'd noted with him.

"Uh," she said, jerking her thumb over her shoulder, "you do realise that the Dome is *that* way?"

Gofreddo blinked several times, and, for the first time since they'd set out from the Dome, Alicia felt a shred of fear in her chest; that Gofreddo might not have all the necessary capacities about him which would enable him to fly this Shuttle to the very best of his abilities. But he cracked through his stone-faced expression with a wry smile.

Then he turned to her.

Locking his brilliant, sky-blue eyes onto hers.

"I did have something else in mind," he said.

———

They flew on for only a few minutes, to a raised dune.

It was then that Alicia noticed that a micro dome had been erected there: one of the portable devices used to support human life. And she realised that it was outfitted with all manner of storage tanks: air, water, and countless others.

She turned into Gofreddo. "What's *this* all about?"

126

"Oh," Gofreddo said, with mock surprise. "This is *top-secret* . . . you're not to tell *anyone* about this, okay?"

He removed one hand from the Shuttle controls, brought his index finger to the tip of her nose.

"All righty," Alicia replied. "I promise." She paused, screwed up her forehead, and looked down over the view. "But what *is* this? I didn't know they were setting up another dome out here."

"It's only temporary," Gofreddo said. "And it's only intended for a single use."

"And what use is that?"

Gofreddo hesitated a long time.

"Oh, come on!" Alicia said, turning in her seat, and unintentionally raising her voice to almost a shout. "You're going to bring me all the way out here—*show me this*—and then you're going to retreat back into your shell all of a sudden?"

Gofreddo held his apprehensive expression another few seconds and then smirked in response.

Alicia gave him a punch on his upper arm, and, as if to spite her, he spun the Shuttle into a ninety-degree position. "Hey!" Alicia cried out, grabbing hold of the sides of her seat and feeling the chest and shoulder straps digging into her skin.

Gofreddo levelled the Shuttle out and brought it downward, headed for the landing pad which served the dome below. "The whole reason for putting this dome together, way out here, is to give the most exclusive—most *valued*—Celestial Stays guests a better view of the lunar eclipse."

Of course she'd heard about the lunar eclipse—she'd had several recipe ideas cross her mind when she had been told about it—but she'd believed that the only place where clients and staff alike would be able to witness it would be from the safety of the Celestial Stays Dome.

Alicia squinted at him. "And there I was believing I was on the inside track when it comes to everything that Celestial Stays dishes out to its clientele—but they kept *this* hidden from me." She snatched a breath. "They told you this because Costantino Zito's your daddy, didn't they?"

Gofreddo gave a slight shrug. "Sometimes being Costantino's son *does* have its benefits." He brought the Shuttle in through the entrance and airlock, before coming to a stop on the landing pad.

As if he'd thoroughly thought this entire matter through, he leaned over to her chair and planted a kiss on her cheek. "Do you want to see what sort of thing they have in store?"

Although Alicia could still feel her skin tingling from where he had kissed her, she did manage to look away from him, and out to the dome.

"It'd be a wasted journey *not* to."

The temporary dome was less spacious than it had seemed from the outside.

She estimated that it was *easily* a thousand times smaller than the Celestial Stays Dome itself. In fact, the dome seemed to have the capacity for—at a push—thirty people.

At least there were around fifteen designated bedrooms.

Just like the Celestial Stays Dome, the outer bubble was completely transparent, so that it afforded a view of the surrounding area. She could make out the Lunar One Monument in the valley below. And then the first rays of sun glimmering on the edge of the horizon.

Before really thinking, she turned on Gofreddo and said, "You know about this place because you're intending to bring your grandmother here, for the eclipse, aren't you?"

Gofreddo blushed slightly, apparently caught out—this seemed to be the only facial expression which he didn't hold complete dominion over.

He gave a bashful shrug.

"We have no idea how long she will last," he said. "It might be that she is too weak to remain until the eclipse—for the eclipse to be her *final* memory." He swallowed hard, and there was a glint of tears in his eyes for a fraction of a moment. "That is why I plan to bring her here—*tomorrow*—so that she will at least have seen her husband for one final time . . ." He turned away from her. "I'm sorry," he said.

Alicia felt a knot form in her throat. She breathed profoundly. Her heart hammered at the underside of her wrists. This seemed so *familiar* . . . something about this was so *familiar* . . .

Finally, she forced her attention back to the dome.

To *inspecting* the dome.

The air, she noted, smelled faintly of strawberries . . . and something else too . . . *champagne?* She allowed herself a wry smile at discovering this little titbit. The bafflement never seemed to be over for her when she turned her mind to consider the high, free-wheeling lives of the wealthy.

As she explored the dome further, she realised that there was one main room—the area which was apparently designated to be the principal viewing area for the lunar eclipse—followed up by a decently-sized kitchen.

It was when she returned from the kitchen that she caught onto the way Gofreddo was looking at her. That he'd brought the sadness which'd pervaded him only a matter of moments ago back under control. However, when all her attention was focussed onto him, he began to inspect his hands; apparently unconsciously channelling his nervous energy into the action. She wondered if he was doing his best to hide his true emotions from her, but he was realising he couldn't do so any longer. That he couldn't hide his emotions from *her*.

"I was just wondering—"

"If I'd do some *baking* for the special event?"

Gofreddo stopped inspecting his hands. He allowed them to fall down at his sides. He met her gaze once again, apparently having pulled himself back together at last. "Yes," he said. "I was thinking that something *sweet* might be very special for an event such as this one . . . such as a lunar eclipse, no?"

Alicia considered this request for several moments, and then she got herself snarled up with those impossibly blue—impossibly *dreamy*—eyes all over again.

"What kind of thing did you have in mind?" she said, taking several unthinking steps toward Gofreddo, and realising that she was far more focussed on his thick, well-blooded lips than the matter of something so *ordinary* as a cake.

"Oh, I am not sure . . ."

However it was clear that he'd not only given the matter a great amount of thought, but that he'd even nailed down some of the finer details. Noting this, Alicia took another few steps toward him, a faint smile now tugging at the corners of her mouth. "Go on," she said. "You can tell me." Now she was within only a few paces of him; she could already feel his body warmth, she breathed his steady, musky scent almost as if it was air. "People tell me that I'm a real *witch* when it comes to the kitchen." She jiggled her fingertips. "Let me conjure up something for you."

Gofreddo's eyes were so wide, and so richly blue, that Alicia was worried she'd become lost in them; that her wits would simply escape her; that she would become a quivering wreck, seeing only that sky-blue, crystalline texture glimmering out at her when she closed her eyes.

She drew breath.

And forced herself to take the next couple of steps.

"Just say the word . . ." she got out, her voice husky—*throaty.*

Now, finally, Gofreddo smiled back.

And she felt his strong, unwavering strength as he coiled his well-muscled arms about her delicate frame. "Why don't you show me what you have in mind *first?*"

The kitchen wasn't large. But it was big enough.

At least for what Alicia had in mind.

Although Gofreddo easily had the strength to overpower her if he so wished, she took great pleasure in being the one to take the lead; the one who had seemed almost to drag Gofreddo under a spell. He was completely in her control.

Alicia was vaguely conscious of the well-sized clay oven—one which must've taken a minor miracle, or else a great deal of money, to bring up here, onto the lunar surface. And she noted the recently sharpened knives which were neatly organised, held onto a wall rack by magnets. Most of all, though, she noted the thick and worn oak surfaces which lined all of the worktop counters . . . because she eased Gofreddo down onto one of them.

And then wrestled with the buttons at the fly of his jeans.

If her fingers weren't magical, then they were at least effortlessly efficient.

Before Gofreddo really knew what'd happened, his jeans lay on the kitchen floor.

Although he reached out for her—clearly wanting to return the favour—she sashayed out of his way. She was clear about this encounter. It might well have been *his* idea to bring them here—to this interstellar equivalent of the proverbial cabin by the lake—but she, sure as hell, was the one who was in charge right now.

With Gofreddo perched on the edge of the oak-topped counter, she took another couple of cautionary steps away from him. First, she slipped off her knee-high boots.

They had served her back home, on the farm, and she had brought them to the Moon as a kind of reminder of what she had left behind on Earth. Instead of being caked in mud, they were lightly lined with fine, white-grey Moon dust.

Her boots dealt with, she teased him, sliding her hands down her thighs, slowly—*gently*—easing the fabric of her dress up her hips.

Slowly revealing her flesh to him.

Her *creamy* flesh.

If there was one thing which Alicia could say for the Moon, it was that it hadn't exactly done wonders for her tan.

As she brought her dress up and over her head—and as she revealed to him that she hadn't been wearing any underwear—she savoured his open-jawed expression.

She *had* been wanting to make an impact, after all.

She toyed with him some more, circling the counter where he sat, naked at the waist, and clearly waiting for her to make the next move.

She came up behind him, crawling her way across the oak surface of the table before bringing her bare arms about his midriff, easing off the leather jacket and then—button by button—undoing the shirt he wore beneath. Before too long he was as naked as she was.

For several minutes, she explored his body with her hands—with her *baker's* hands.

She felt the ripped muscles, and she wondered how he had got them; if they'd been won through hard-headed, monotonous discipline at the gym, or if they were the mere symptom of an adventurous life well lived.

When she came across a barely healed scar—slightly to the left of his belly button—she thought she had her answer.

She felt his breathing. His body filling with air.

And then deflating.

His muscles burgeoning, flexing.

And then relaxing.

In-between these rotations was when Alicia knew she had her chance.

When Alicia knew *she* held the advantage.

So she bided her time.

Waited for her opportunity.

And then *jumped* him.

18

VARYING PRIORITIES

*I*t was a minor miracle that Alicia managed to wake up.

And when she did she had the sun in her eyes.

Although it was mitigated by the ultra-violet filter of the dome —so that its strength was rendered a little weaker than it was back on Earth—it was bright enough to cause her to become lost in the dazzle. She brought her hand up to shield her eyes from the glare and took swift stock of her surroundings.

She was here.

Still here.

In the dome which overlooked the Lunar One Monument.

She glanced about her, trying to pin down 'here' a little more exactly.

Well, they'd left the kitchen—and their clothes—behind, that much was obvious.

She realised now that they had ended up in the main viewing area.

She was lying on her side, her body bare beside Gofreddo's.

Through the windows, she made out the lunar plains stretching for miles and miles and miles, wrapping around the horizon. She held very still, realising that the only sound she could hear was from Gofreddo's gentle breathing.

As she stared out across the plains, a strange, imaginary panic struck her.

She recalled the dream she'd been having.

She'd dreamed that she and Gofreddo had stared up into the lunar sky, watching on as the last of human habitation left them behind. Stranding them here, on the surface of the Moon, forevermore.

She breathed in deeply, taking the air right down to the pit of her stomach.

And she realised that, really, she didn't care anymore.

For the first time in maybe *forever* she felt content.

Happy.

She turned her attention down onto Gofreddo.

He slept on his back, with his arm sprawled across his chest. As always, his blond hair stuck up in tufts. She made out the fine, downy blond hair which ran from his belly button all the way down . . . well, he had a blanket they'd snaffled from one of the bedrooms draped across his waist now; keeping him from showing off anything he preferred to keep *private*.

Gofreddo woke with a start.

His shoulders became tense.

He propped himself up on his elbows.

He reached for his temples as if he had a migraine coming on.

"What . . . what *time* is it?" he said, screwing up his eyes.

"Uh," Alicia replied, reaching her finger into her earpiece, and then realising that here—*all the way out here*—there was no connection to the Link. "Don't know," she finally answered.

"*Shit!*" Gofreddo said, scrabbling his way back up onto his feet.

He glanced about, as if the surrounding world might be able to provide the answers.

While he did all this glancing, he allowed the blanket to drop down, about his feet, and Alicia caught a decent eyeful. Beginning to feel a little self-conscious, she reached out for the discarded blanket and subtly dragged it over herself.

"Have you got somewhere to be?" she said, her voice a touch dreamy, from where she still lay—*naked*—on her side at Gofreddo's feet.

"Where're my clothes?" he said.

"Try the kitchen," she replied, seeing that he was well and truly stumped by his search efforts.

With a smart—*efficient*—smile, he disappeared.

She heard him rooting about noisily before he emerged from the kitchen doorway, now dressed in his shirt and jeans, if looking just a *touch* ruffled. He clutched his bundled-up leather jacket to his chest. Shaking his head, he said, "Jesus, what did we *do* in there last night?"

Alicia arched an eyebrow. "I'm sure it'll all come back eventually."

Apparently getting over his shock, he worked his jacket over his shoulders, taking care to poke both his arms through the sleeves. "I've got to . . . got to . . ."

"Go?" Alicia said, again deciding to help him out.

"*Yes*," Gofreddo replied, looking even more rushed and frantic now.

He made for the landing pad.

He'd almost got right out of the door before Alicia decided that she *really should* say something . . . otherwise they might get themselves into some trouble further down the line.

"I think you're forgetting something," she said.

"Huh, what?" Gofreddo spun around on his heel. He near enough *glared* at her, no doubt challenging her to make him even more stressed than he clearly already was.

Finally it seemed to strike him—and, perhaps, some of the details of the previous night returned. "Oh, right! *Shit!*" he added for good measure, this time with a smile creeping across his lips.

Alicia felt her chest tighten as he stepped toward her.

It was strange. Even though she'd had countless intimate encounters with near-strangers, she hardly ever got to feeling nervous; like she did now.

Did that mean Gofreddo wasn't a stranger?

He crouched down before her, leaned into her lips, and pressed his mouth—warm and sweet—up against hers. With a smile, he straightened up and said, "You'd probably better get your clothes— I don't want to make more of a spectacle than we already did."

As Alicia rose up, she couldn't help grinning too.

The trip back in the Shuttle was uneventful.

Neither one of them said anything.

It seemed like, the night before, they'd said everything that needed to be said.

As Gofreddo drifted the Shuttle down toward Entry Clearance, and the landing pad, she felt his hand reach out and press up against her own. It was almost as if sparks bounced through her blood.

Her heartbeat hummed in her ears.

This really *did* feel like the start of something.

. . . Or was she just deluding herself?

When Gofreddo brought the Shuttle down into the landing bay, alongside all the other parked-up Shuttles, Alicia was glad to find that the hangar was empty . . . that there was no sign of the other pilots. She couldn't quite have faced it if there'd been a whole group of fist-pumping male cheerleaders, as happened in innumerable movies.

Then again, she didn't believe that Gofreddo was the type.

That he wasn't the type to go bragging to his friends . . . in fact, Alicia caught onto the sneaking suspicion that Gofreddo really didn't have many close friends at all . . .

She supposed that was one of the prices of fame and fortune.

One never knew just what people's motivations truly were.

Even though there wasn't any sort of welcoming committee, Alicia couldn't say that she felt all that wild about having to catch a PEAR back wearing the dress she'd been in the night before. She supposed that if she'd had enough foresight—and, to be honest, a girl like herself really *should* have—then she would've packed an overnight bag.

Then again, this theoretical 'overnight bag' would hardly have been all that subtle to lug along on the lunar Shuttle . . .

Gofreddo dealt her a hurried but passionate kiss before rushing off in the direction of a doorway marked 'Locker Room'. Alicia waited until he'd disappeared around the corner, and she supposed that he was going to take a quick shower and get changed into his flight overalls for his grandmother's visit to the Lunar One Monument.

Although Alicia would've liked nothing more than to subtly slip her way into the Locker Room and materialise behind the wet, warm and *naked* Gofreddo, she appreciated that his thoughts were no doubt on other things now. On his grandmother.

So Alicia caught a PEAR to the Basements, took a quick

shower, got changed into her daily work overalls and then turned up at the Orbital Café.

She was glad to find that Kyra had battened down the hatches, and made it so that Alicia arriving more than an hour late wasn't an issue.

Alicia quickly threw an apron on over her overalls and got to work, looking over the shoulders of her kitchen staff, ensuring that nobody was stepping out of line in any big way. And apart from a couple of minor alterations—some observations she made about stray flour or dough, or other ingredients—there wasn't all that much input she needed to give.

Once she'd got through with her supervisory duties, she took a quick peek out into the customer area and saw that, for the most part, the whole place was deserted; only the odd couple here and there keeping the tables and chairs company.

She allowed herself a satisfied exhale when she returned to the kitchen, and then she glanced to Kyra, who was surreptitiously standing to one side.

Although it looked as if Kyra was calm and collected, as if she'd hardly batted an eyelash all morning, Alicia knew—from personal experience—that looks could very easily be deceiving.

And, above all, that when organisation looked effortless it often meant that a large amount of blood, sweat, and/or tears had been expelled in order to get results.

Acting on impulse, Alicia leaned forward and embraced Kyra.

She squeezed the unwitting girl to her chest.

Thought she could feel the confusion seeping out of her pores.

But Alicia wasn't quite done yet.

"Thank you," she said, leaning in to whisper in Kyra's ear.

Once Alicia had let her go, she couldn't help noting the

confused expression which lined Kyra's face . . . however hard she attempted to hide it with a nervous grin.

It was then that Alicia recalled her discussion with Gofreddo the night before . . . the *unusually frank* discussion they'd had in the kitchen . . . just before clothes had been cast off.

He had asked her if she would prepare something for the lunar eclipse, if she would put something together for the celebration; for what might well prove to be his grandmother's final moments *alive*.

"Kyra?" Alicia said. "When is the lunar eclipse?"

Kyra, it seemed, was somewhere stuck between delirium and an eagerness to please. "Next week," she replied. "Next *Wednesday*."

"And what day is it today?"

"Saturday."

Alicia counted off the days before Wednesday. "Three days," she said, looking back into Kyra's eyes. "Three *days* till the eclipse."

Kyra nodded in reply.

That wasn't much time for Alicia to carry out her research. She thought back to Gofreddo, about how much of a big deal it must've been for him to reach the point where he could *trust* her . . . and now Alicia realised that she had the chance to pay the compliment forward; to place her trust in someone else.

In Kyra.

Alicia looked back at her. "Would you be able to do some research for me? It's something I need done, ahead of the lunar eclipse. At the Armstrong Archive. Where I pulled the files on Estonian cuisine last time, you remember?"

"Of course," Kyra replied.

"I mean," Alicia continued, "if you're willing to give me a looser rein . . . as long as you're fairly sure I'm not going to flip out or anything?"

Kyra smiled wider. "I think that can be arranged," she said. "When I spoke with Mackenzie, she seemed to think that by the end of next week I shall be reassigned." She held out a mock admonishing finger, waggled it at Alicia's nose. "Just don't go and do anything crazy for a few days, then this should all be over with."

"Okay," Alicia said, "then I'd like you to pull any files you can on Argentinian cooking—particularly the *sweet* stuff, you know, the kind of foods that you would eat at a wedding, or a birthday party."

She resisted the urge to say 'wake', although that was closer to the truth.

Kyra gave a smile, nodded, and then headed out of the room.

Alicia glanced over her kitchen staff, to Drake, Stéphanie and Millat.

They all continued to work, like well-oiled gears in a machine.

Feeling a yawn coming on, Alicia decided to take a quick trip outside, to catch some of the fresh Dome air. As she stood outside, leaning up against the faux-Alpine façade, she became hypnotised by the constant comings and goings of the PEARS.

She tracked them as they swooped through the air, on their way to their destinations, only truly known to their occupants.

Alicia supposed she'd been outside for about five minutes when she noted one of the PEARs approaching the Orbital Café landing pad. Already, she attempted to make out the occupants. She supposed that there were more guests on their way. More orders. After the marvellous night last night, she was right back to day-to-day life with a bump.

But, then again, there wasn't all that much normal about life on the Moon.

Life beneath the Celestial Stays Dome.

However, when the PEAR came to a halt and the visor swept back, she immediately realised that it wasn't a guest within.

Instead of the burgundy overalls which guests were compelled to wear, the occupants of the PEAR wore jet-black.

The black overalls of the Security Division.

Alicia's eyes quickly shifted onto the features.

One male.

One female.

The male she didn't recognise.

The female she *did*.

It was Lan Niu.

Despite knowing her name, Alicia wouldn't even say that she was so much as an acquaintance. She had only truly grown to know *who* she was through Louise. Because of what Louise had gone through . . .

Lan had black plaits and *blacker* eyes, all of which matched her *black* Security overalls.

Throughout her time beneath the Celestial Stays Dome, Alicia had had very few run-ins with Security. Just as when she'd been back on Earth, she knew how to keep her nose clean; how to follow the rules . . . or, perhaps more accurately, how to bend or break the rules without being spotted. It was Lan who spoke to Alicia.

"Guardian Brennan," she said, her voice short, sharp and clipped.

"What's the matter?"

"I've got orders to bring you to a meeting with Supervisor Habiba Nuha."

Alicia's heart clenched.

She felt a chill pass through her blood.

"What is this . . ."

But before Alicia could get out any more words, Lan and the male member of the Security team took hold of her elbows, strong arming her in the direction of the PEAR.

Supervisor Habiba Nuha's office was located on the ground floor of the Lunar Grand.

Near to the kitchens.

As the Supervisor of Catering this only made sense, since the largest-scale operation beneath the Celestial Stays Dome took place within the kitchens of the Lunar Grand.

Although the Orbital Café fell under the Division of Catering, it was very much seen as being solely beneath Alicia's command. That said, when she needed to check in with someone, then it was Supervisor Habiba.

Normally, Alicia wouldn't have been fazed by the prospect of a meeting with Supervisor Habiba—there simply would be no reason for it—but, then again, she'd never previously been frog-marched here . . . or *anywhere* for that matter.

And so she couldn't help but feel that this meeting had some sort of a disciplinary element to it.

She was at least glad that the members of the Security Division had seen fit to release her before she'd set foot in the office. And that they'd deigned only to linger in the doorway while Alicia undertook her meeting with Supervisor Habiba.

Supervisor Habiba's office featured many pieces of cooking paraphernalia: wooden spoons, milk jugs, and a couple of chopping boards which hung down off the walls. All of these items, Alicia supposed had been specially selected by Habiba when she had travelled to the Moon from Earth.

Habiba herself was sat at her desk, hands clutched before her, considering Alicia. As always, Alicia was struck by her handsome cheekbones, and how her walnut-coloured eyes constantly peered over the tops of her half-moon glasses. Without fail, Alicia was impressed by how *in control* Habiba always seemed . . . a quality which Alicia assumed she had acquired after decades and decades spent in the catering business.

From Alicia's own experience, she knew that the most successful in the field were always—almost without a doubt—those who had the ability to keep their heads when all those about them were losing theirs. Alicia had always thought herself to possess this ability.

What marked Supervisor Habiba's office out all the more was how the wallpaper behind the chair looked out over the Lunar Grand kitchens. Alicia briefly glanced over Supervisor Habiba's shoulder and caught sight of the myriad of activity taking place beyond.

All those people working tirelessly for the guests.

All of them squeezing a tiny piece of their soul into their work.

Putting their *passion* into the flavour of the food.

Alicia brought her attention back to Habiba.

"Please," she said, with a slight smile. "Take a seat, Alicia."

Alicia looked to the chairs located just before Habiba's desk.

There were two of them.

Somehow she wondered if it might be a test.

If she was supposed to pick one or the other.

In the end, she chose the one on the left, and immediately began to regret her choice as it gave her an unobstructed view into the Lunar Grand's kitchens.

It would be nothing but a distraction for the meeting.

Drawing on her powers of concentration, she turned her attention onto Habiba. From somewhere, Alicia managed to produce a smile. "I'm sorry about the manner in which you were brought here, Alicia, but it's all down to protocol, you understand?"

For the first time, Alicia felt truly afraid.

This was all so *official* sounding.

"What protocol?" she managed to get out, her voice a touch shaky now.

Habiba stretched a grin across her lips. "Well, we have intelligence which suggests your unauthorised exit—followed by your unauthorised *entrance*—to the Dome." Apparently receiving cues from her earpiece, Habiba continued, "The exit concerned was last night, while the entrance was"—here she eyed Alicia closely—"*this morning.*"

Alicia suddenly felt an itchy sensation take hold just beneath the surface of her skin.

A whole batch of fire-ant eggs had hatched all at once.

"I . . . I . . ." she got out, before Habiba held up a flat palm for her to stop.

The image put Alicia in mind of a policeman directing traffic.

"Protocol is protocol, Alicia, you understand that," Habiba said. "Which is why I've been forced to put you on a written warning."

" 'A *written* warning' ?" Alicia blurted out.

Habiba nodded dolefully. "It's my understanding that, a few weeks ago, you were involved in a, uh, *situation* concerning another member of staff—a fellow Celestial Stays employee?"

Alicia supposed Habiba was referencing her assault on Julius.

She decided that, right now, there was nothing for her to do but suck up her punishment and try not to put a foot wrong. It took a great deal of inner strength, but she managed to button her lip.

Habiba continued, "I believe it's my responsibility as your superior—as well as your *friend* to tell you that I spent a good deal of time with Supervisor Angliss discussing your situation."

Alicia felt a tingle pass through her blood to think about Mackenzie Angliss, Supervisor of Human Resources, *personally* discussing her situation as if she was some kind of junior upstart.

"I managed to convince her," Habiba went on, "that you are still the best prospect for managing the Orbital Café, and that, apart from this written warning, you should be allowed to carry on as normal—just knowing that . . ."

"A third strike and I'm out?"

Habiba gave a solemn nod.

"Okay," Alicia said, "that sounds fair." She paused for a long while, distracted by the workings of the Lunar Grand kitchens behind Habiba.

She couldn't help but wonder what it must be like to have command of a kitchen like that. To be the one who could painstakingly construct the daily dishes; have the final say about presentation and flavour . . . and for so many distinguished guests . . .

"Listen, Alicia." This time Habiba leaned over her desk, and took hold of one of Alicia's hands, in an apparent gesture of the highest intimacy. "I still believe that you're the one to take over from me, when the time comes, but there're others to convince. There're others who believe there're better candidates." She gave a shake of her head and removed her hand from where it lay on top of Alicia's. "And, to be honest, there's only so much influence *I* have . . . since I won't be very much accountable for the decision— *you're* the one *they'll* have to live with."

Again, Alicia lost herself to the busy, ant nest-like activity occurring in the Lunar Grand kitchens over Habiba's shoulder. Finally, she looked Habiba in the eye once again.

Managed to raise a smile.

"I'll take care, from now on," Alicia said. "I'll think carefully before I do anything."

Habiba smiled back.

Rose up out of her chair.

"Good," she said. "That's *good* . . ."

Alicia padded toward the door, conscious of not dragging this awkward meeting out any longer than it had to go. When she got to the door, she noted that the two members of the Security Division were still there. She caught Lan's eye.

As she was about to walk away, she couldn't resist the final, parting shot.

Over her shoulder, she said, "I guess I'm not getting shot of my spy anytime soon?"

"Your spy?"

"*Kyra*," Alicia replied, spitting her name as if they hadn't kissed and made up what seemed like an age ago.

Habiba stood stock-still.

Shook her head.

"I'm afraid all of that is really Mackenzie Angliss's area—I don't know much about it."

Alicia knew that Habiba was telling the truth.

But it didn't make it hurt any less.

All the same, Alicia managed to get free of Habiba's office without further showdowns.

It surprised Alicia somewhat when the two members of the Security Division ordered the PEAR back to the Orbital Café. She'd somehow assumed that she would be automatically relieved of her duties for the shift. Then again, she wasn't going to complain about *not* getting any more detention.

As she hopped out of the PEAR, feeling glad to get her personal space back to herself, something at the back of her mind tickled her.

She turned around.

Caught Lan Niu in her sights.

Tilted her head to one side.

"Can I have a word?" Alicia said.

Lan, although apparently taken aback by this request, didn't see fit to reject it.

And she left the male member behind, apparently not needing him to watch her back with a psychopath like Alicia Brennan around.

Lan remained straight-faced, her expression as cold as she could make it.

Alicia was direct.

And she was sure not to beat about the bush.

If there was anything she'd learned about dealing with Security, it was that they didn't appreciate wishy-washy inference. They liked to have everything put directly, and they would answer in kind.

"Listen," Alicia said, "that scan—or whatever systems you used to detect my entrance and exit from the Dome. Didn't you see anybody else with me?"

If Lan had anything at all to give away, she didn't show any reaction.

Her expression remained neutral.

Acting on impulse, Alicia reached out and touched Lan on her forearm. She looked Lan straight in the eye. "Please," she said. "I need to know."

It wasn't any more than the flicker of an eyelash, but it told

Alicia everything she needed; that there was more to this than first appeared.

She released Lan.

Lan gave her what could only be described as a 'professional nod' and then trod her way back to the waiting PEAR.

Alicia stood still for several moments.

She felt a throbbing pulse pass through her veins.

Her heart once more *thud-thudding* in her eardrums.

And she told herself not to be angry.

19

DELAYED REUNION

*E*ven as *Gofreddo* brought them down upon the Lunar One Monument, he could feel himself trembling all over. He had hoped that visiting his grandfather's resting place with Alicia might mitigate the onrushing emotion he now felt, but—*evidently* —he'd been wrong.

It was all he could do to bring the Shuttle in gently to the landing pad.

He helped Wendy with his grandmother's wheelchair. Between the two of them, they brought her down to the ground level using the Shuttle's access lift.

Apparently seeing that he was shaken up, Wendy took it upon herself to wheel his grandmother along the flattened path leading up to the Monument.

He hadn't been this close with Alicia, of course.

They had only flown over the tight, protective bubble which served to house the Lunar One Monument; to provide a habitable micro environment for human beings.

Although Gofreddo had managed to rankle access to the dome which sat just up the valley, overlooking this site, it was another matter entirely to gain access to the Lunar One memorial bubble. And, of course, temporary access had been granted him and his grandmother. Wendy, too.

When Gofreddo had first learned about this restricted access, he'd wondered if it was some sort of measure put in place to minimise the risk of vandalism, but, in the end, he decided that it had more to do with reverence.

That the appropriate authorities had decided that the site's sanctity should be protected at all costs. It shouldn't become a simple day trip.

Gofreddo wondered if—when he had visited the site with his father—there had been special access granted because of their familial connection. Because it was his father's father, and Gofreddo's grandfather, who'd been buried on this very spot.

It seemed that, with each step Gofreddo took, he became heavier.

The journey became more difficult.

He gently sketched his mind back to his first visit here.

He'd been hungover, as far as he could remember. He'd no doubt been wearing a pair of sunglasses to hide the dark circles which clung to the bottoms of his eyes. What might his grandfather have thought of him?

What sort of *respect* had he shown him?

It was when Gofreddo was within only a few paces of the monument—when he looked upon the cylindrical form of Lunar One depicted by the sculpture—that he felt he absolutely *shouldn't* be here. That he didn't *deserve* to be here.

He glanced to his grandmother, seeing her nestled in her

wheelchair, all bundled up with blankets as Wendy stood stoically by.

He searched his grandmother's face for any sign of emotion.

For *tears*.

He had expected her to be deeply affected by the sight.

But . . . she seemed to be taking it coolly, calmly.

Gofreddo shifted a glance back off to the Shuttle, waiting for them outside the bubble, on the landing pad. He *itched* to get back into the pilot's seat. To find himself back behind the controls. Everything was much easier when he was sat up in the cockpit. He had something to occupy his mind. He had only to follow the flight plan, monitor the dials and gauges, just . . .

It was then that his grandmother turned in her chair.

When she met Gofreddo's eye.

And, seemingly against the solemn tension which hung in the air, she gave him a smile.

She angled her head back to Wendy.

Apparently having spent enough time in one another's company to be able to communicate without words, Wendy wheeled Gofreddo's grandmother away from the Monument. Toward him.

It was difficult to explain.

How Gofreddo felt so much fear at the prospect of an old woman being wheeled toward him. He who had come through a childhood beleaguered by paparazzi, and by unseen threats of kidnap, the ever-present prospect of being made a fool by wily fraudsters.

And now he was afraid of one of the few people he knew in his life to be genuine.

To be worthy of his *trust*.

He wanted to run.

To run back to the Shuttle.

But he stood his ground.

Met her eyes.

"*Nieto*," she said, reaching up for him from her wheelchair.

Gofreddo bent at the knees, crouching down over her so that she could brush her fingertips against his cheek.

"I am so sorry you never knew the truth," she said.

Gofreddo's stomach sunk.

It ashamed him to think that he had felt anger about this— that he had felt some kind of *betrayal* at having this enormous piece of family history hidden from him. How he had been unable to see the people around him for what they truly were. *Humans*.

Fallible.

"Being a pilot—being an *adventurer*. You would have made him so proud," she said, her palm still cupping his cheek.

Although Gofreddo was aware of Wendy looming just behind the wheelchair, he couldn't recall a greater moment of intimacy between himself and his grandmother.

"Thank you," Gofreddo just about managed to get out.

With that, his grandmother's frail hand fell away from his cheek, returning to her lap.

She bowed her head, as if this trip had drained her strength.

Wendy, again without the need for a word to be spoken between them, took the signal to wheel his grandmother back toward the Shuttle.

For a long time, Gofreddo stood still, aware of the Lunar One Monument just ahead of him but refusing to look at it.

In the end, he turned his back without looking.

He was determined that his grandmother would see the lunar eclipse.

That she would have a final chance to say goodbye before slipping from this plane of existence.

2 0

PREFERENTIAL TREATMENT

licia was determined not to lose her head.

She had made the point to herself—very clearly, *unambiguously*—that she would approach this situation in a cool, calm, businesslike manner.

Because, after all was said and done, she was a serious businesswoman.

The Orbital Café would've flopped if she hadn't been.

To prepare herself for the meeting, she'd taken a couple of hours after her shift had ended to have a dip in the swimming pool followed by a session in the sauna. She felt as though she had stretched and flexed every muscle in her body, and then gone and sweated out just as much as she could conceivably manage. It escaped her to think of a time when she had *ever* been more relaxed in all her life.

. . . Perhaps there was that *one* time when she'd visited that Turkish bathhouse, but that, really, was a whole other story . . .

She paced up to the door, wearing her royal-blue Celestial

155

Stays overalls. She felt neat and prim—*authoritative*—to have the silver Guardian badge sewn on at the breast pocket. When she came to think of it, she *outranked* Gofreddo, so what she was worried about, she truly didn't have so much as an idea.

She had looked up Gofreddo Zito in the Link directory and found no entry.

This was surely an attempt on his behalf to fly under the radar.

When she'd searched for 'Freddy Z', though, she'd been in luck.

And it'd led her here.

She took another second to compose herself before she smartly rapped her knuckles against the door. Then she stood back and waited, knowing that, even if she hadn't knocked, Gofreddo's earpiece would've informed him that there was someone at the door.

Still, she was a farm girl at heart.

Even now technology felt alien—somewhat *unfeeling*.

The door slid back and Gofreddo appeared there.

She noted, right away, that he looked somewhat dishevelled.

That he had obviously not had a chance to shave.

She knew, of course, that he had gone out to the Lunar One Monument with his grandmother, and so she hadn't expected him to be all *up* and enthusiastic.

But neither had she been expecting him to look like death warmed up.

He did manage to dig out a smile for her, though.

Albeit a *weary* one.

He leaned in for a kiss, and not seeing any reason to deny him, she kissed him back. Nothing more than the brush of lips. Alicia wondered what he might read about her mood from the kiss, or if he was too tired to take observations, draw conclusions.

Somehow, she couldn't quite imagine that Gofreddo Zito *ever* got too tired to be anything but calculating—*exacting*.

"Come in," he said, backing away from her, near enough whispering the words.

Alicia did as he said.

She neatly stepped into his apartment.

The first thing which struck her about the apartment was that it was—for all intents and purposes—one-hundred-per-cent identical to her own. Although she didn't have a clear idea of what she'd had in mind, she had *at least* thought it would be double the size of her own.

The second thing she noted was the mess.

It looked like the proverbial 'bomb' had hit it.

Clothes were screwed up and bundled about the floor.

Some of the luckier items—among them, Alicia noticed, the leather jacket—had been hung off the back of chairs or slung from the headboard of the bed.

As the door slipped shut, sealing the two of them inside, Alicia instinctively turned back where she met those almost overpowering, silvery-blue eyes.

"Excuse the mess," Gofreddo said, slipping past her. "I didn't know I was going to have company." He bent over and set about collecting up dirty flight overalls which lay scattered about the floor, tossing them into the laundry chute in the corner of the room as he went.

She wanted to tell him not to bother, that she had only come here for a brief chat, but somehow he seemed to be better off with some form of task to occupy his body and mind.

More *purposeful*.

She thought of asking after the day's trip to the Lunar One Monument, but decided against it, thinking that it really wasn't her place. No, she was better off stating her business and getting out.

"I got in trouble today," she said.

At this, Gofreddo straightened up. He seemed to forget about the dirty laundry he'd gathered in his arms for a couple of moments before he snapped back to the present and tossed the contents into the chute, after the rest of the soiled clothing.

"What sort of trouble?" he said, turning his back to her as he worked to clear one of the chairs.

"A meeting with my Supervisor—Habiba Nuha."

As Gofreddo set about prodding a coat hanger into the sleeves of the leather jacket, and then eyed up the rack—apparently its final destination—he frowned to himself. "What was the meeting about?"

Alicia took a steady breath.

She could feel herself trembling.

Despite all her best efforts—despite all the trouble she'd gone to so that she would be calm—she could feel herself beginning to tremble.

Against all odds, she kept her voice straight.

"It was about my unauthorised exit—and *re-entrance*—to the Dome."

Gofreddo slipped the leather jacket onto the rack. Then he settled his hands on his hips, and seemed to look at her with his full concentration for the first time.

" 'Unauthorised' ?" he repeated.

Now he reached up and held his hand to his temple.

Perhaps he had a headache.

A shame . . . that would only make this all the more difficult for him.

Alicia nodded, and then continued, "I'm on a second strike—

next time I screw something up they'll have me demoted from my position at the Orbital Café." Noticing that a coil of her fringe had sprung free of her tightly bound bun, she reached up and flipped it out of her eyes. "Have me pot-washing in the Lunar Grand kitchens, no doubt."

Gofreddo's lips parted.

He blinked several times as if this was some kind of a bad dream.

She wondered if he was having trouble taking on board just what this meant—*understanding* the implications of what this would mean to a 'normal' person like Alicia. It wasn't like she could call up her daddy and have him sort her out with a job piloting lunar Shuttles.

"I . . . I . . . wasn't *thinking*," Gofreddo said, breaking off eye contact, and his gaze slipping to the floor, which was still covered in dirty laundry.

"Well," Alicia said, "I don't *blame* you for it; nothing like that." She pursed her lips, already feeling as if her throat was contracting. But she knew that she had to continue with what she had to say. She had to *force* herself to the end. "Listen, Gofreddo," she said. "What happened last night, it was *fun* . . . and it's been, I don't know, an *experience* to hang around with you, but I need to think about my career. I need to think about where *I'm* going."

Seemingly still struck by a daze, he turned his attention up to her. " 'Hanging around' ?" he said.

She expected to hear a touch of anger there.

She had purposefully chosen that phrase while she'd been thinking things over in the sauna. She had designed it so that it might bring out some sort of an aggressive response in him. And that would only make the breaking-off process easier.

At least in the present.

But Gofreddo didn't seem angry at all.

It was the very worst of those reactions—as teachers and parents would often poke and prod at.

He was *disappointed.*

Finally, he turned his attention back to her. "I am very sorry you feel that way," he said. "It was an innocent mistake, I can tell you that."

"Yes, well," Alicia said, unable to keep the sigh out of her voice, "some of us are playing by different rules; some of us don't receive preferential treatment."

With a shake of his head, he snapped his gaze back onto hers. "Okay," he said, and then added, "okay, okay," as if he was validating her feelings before he pulled the whole shining-white-knight routine. "I'll look into this—I'll see *why* I was overlooked for the punishment . . . I shall . . ."

But Alicia couldn't help interrupting him.

She shook her head.

"Don't you see?" she said. "It's all a waste of time . . . how're they going to punish *you,* the son of Costantino Zito?"

Here she noted a touch of colour enter Gofreddo's cheeks.

Perhaps, finally, she *was* getting to him.

Maybe she was stoking a fire in his blood.

Turning him against her.

This might be easier than she'd thought.

She continued, "Even if they sack you—if you get yourself unceremoniously stuffed into the next tin can headed back to Earth—you'll have more prospects down there, waiting for you. I'm sure if the worst came to the worst your *dad* would give you a job." She shrugged. "Others of us—others like *me*—we've put a lot of time and effort into building a career." Here she eyed him closely, sure now that he was rising to the bait. "If you think I'm prepared to throw all that away because of some *fling* then you're sadly mistaken."

Silence dominated the room now.

She waited for Gofreddo to tell her to get out, or words to that effect.

But he simply stood where he was, looking worn-out, down-trodden . . . as if he had any right—*any right at all*—to look or feel that way.

"I'll be going then," Alicia said, turning her back on him.

And although he didn't fly into a rage, attempt to prevent her leaving, he did nothing to stop her from going either.

WILFUL PASSIONS

single droplet of sweat rolled down the side of Alicia's face. She reached up and wiped it away with the back of her hand.

Then she turned her attention back downward, to the mixing bowl; to the task she was currently working on. She pulled her hands free of the dough then sighed, long and hard.

For some reason she just couldn't get it right.

She just couldn't get the *consistency* right.

It should've been so easy, there wasn't anything more complicated about putting together the batter than flour, eggs, sugar and margarine. And yet it was either coming out far too dry—far too *floury*—or emerging in the form of a slick-and-slimy, good-for-nothing paste.

Knowing herself—knowing that whenever she forced herself to 'power on' at something without thinking it always led to the same results—she took a deep breath and then a physical step back from the mixing bowl.

Despite having put some distance between her and the bowl, she couldn't help but stare into the mixture, considering just what it was that'd gone wrong.

With her floury hands, she reached up and batted her fringe out of her eyes.

She was alone here, in the kitchen. And it was well past the end of her shift. But, like always when she had a deadline for some event looming, she put in extra hours. Although she might've had a falling-out with Gofreddo, that didn't mean she was about to call off her participation in the lunar eclipse catering.

What she was doing now she liked to call Preparation and Practice. It was how she termed the time it took her to perfect her recipes. It was her belief that the most important thing for her, while she was cooking, was to have the ability to *not* think about the dish she was creating . . . that was, she always aimed to reach the stage where she could create the dish by heart.

It allowed her mind to wander onto higher-level details such as presentation, more subtle flavouring and, arguably most important of all, diner satisfaction and feedback so that she could work toward perfecting not only the recipe but the process itself.

Once she *had* got a recipe right then she would have it documented so that her kitchen staff could follow it casily. It seemed like an awful lot of pressure to put on herself because if she documented a recipe before it was ready then a mistake could quite easily become engrained in the process of many employees.

"Getting hot and bothered in here?"

A shudder ran down Alicia's spine.

She glanced up.

Saw that Louise stood in the doorway.

She eased away the grimace which'd sprung up onto her lips. "Hi," she said.

"*Hi*," Louise answered back, treading between the preparation tables and approaching Alicia. She nodded to the mixing bowl. "What's that you've got there?"

"Isn't it obvious?"

Louise shrugged a shoulder. "Sorry, I've always been something of a dunce when it comes to cooking. Guess that's what I get for being an office monkey, then gardener, doesn't exactly put me in good stead for being any sort of domestic goddess, I suppose. Poor Njhay."

"Yeah," Alicia replied, turning her attention back to the mixing bowl. " 'Poor Njhay'."

Men were really the last thing she wanted to think about right now.

The lunar eclipse was due to take place the evening after next and she was determined to not only be ready for it, but to *eclipse* the eclipse with the Argentine cuisine she was preparing.

With what felt like the thousandth sigh of the evening, Alicia forced herself to turn her attention away from the mixing bowl and onto Louise. "This is a *pastafrola*, or"—she halted for a moment, picking out a hair she spotted in amongst the flour—"it will be in about an hour or so's time."

"Interesting," Louise said, leaning over the mixing bowl and pouting before switching her gaze back onto Alicia. "And what's a *'pastafrola'* when it's at home?"

"Kind of like a jam tart," Alicia said. "It has a lattice-like topping. Tasty," she added with a quick, insincere smile.

Louise shifted her gaze off to the rest of the counter, to the other dishes which Alicia had prepared beforehand and had ready to plump in the oven or else leave in the fridge overnight for tasting tomorrow morning. "And what're those?" Louise asked.

"The doughy rolls with *dulce de leche* are called *piononos*. The *tortas fritas* are the fried dough things that look and taste *kind* of like battered pancakes. Those white-and-dark, double-layered chocolate biscuits on that baking tray there are called *afajores*. The last one is"—Alicia stretched her mind for the name of the dish —"*Budín de pan*," she got out, finally, and then rolled her eyes at her scattered brain. "Bread pudding."

Louise puffed out her cheeks. "My, oh my, you really are in the mood to impress."

Although it wasn't anything out of the ordinary for there to be some playful back-and-forth between her and Louise, Alicia found that right here—*right now*—it really rubbed her up the wrong way. "Why'd you say that?" Alicia asked, trying to sound casual, as she dunked her fingers back into the doomed mixture destined for the *pastafrola*.

"It's just a lot of effort."

"Nah," Alicia replied, finally feeling that she'd got the consistency of the *pastafrola* mixture right this time. "No effort at all." She paused, dipping her index finger in to check whether it would stick. "When you've got a passion it's not work at all."

Louise breathed out sharply. "Wow," she said. "That's told me."

Despite being fully aware of the biting tone she was treating Louise to, Alicia didn't feel much in an apologetic mood. She set about wedging the *pastafrola* into the shape she wanted it and then got to work stirring the filling—guava jelly she'd managed to dig out of a long-forgotten, quite dusty, tin can in the pantry.

Alicia wanted nothing more than for Louise to leave her alone now.

For Louise to simply *catch a clue* and leave her to her cooking.

Allow her to calm herself down.

But Louise was, apparently, in an insistent mood.

"So, I take it that your Latin love affair hasn't come to fruition?"

Alicia felt her whole body go rigid, but she tried her best not to communicate the sensation with her tone of voice. "You could say that it was *rotten* from the start."

"How so?"

The way Louise asked the question was so casual. That was the thing about Louise; how she managed to make even the heaviest subject sound as if it was something to be lightly discussed over tea and cakes. She could see how Louise had made such a success of herself during her corporate career.

"Look," Alicia said, working to mould the lattice for the *pastafrola*, "let's just say that when two people come from disparate backgrounds; when a couple of people are coming from *entirely* different cultures and contexts, there's almost no chance of getting it to work."

Louise shrugged. "I don't know, it seems to work fine for me and Njhay."

"Yeah, well"—Alicia gave the current lattice an extra-hard battering with the heel of her hand—"that's *you* and *Njhay*."

"You make it sound as if we were star-crossed lovers."

"You were, weren't you?"

"Far from it."

Alicia allowed Louise's final remark to drift into silence.

She *really* wasn't in the mood to discuss this stuff.

Not right now.

Or perhaps *ever*.

"Why don't you tell me what he did wrong?" Louise said, her voice finally cutting through the quiet like a broken piece of glass.

Alicia was taken off-guard by the directness of the question.

And she really wasn't sure how to answer.

So she just busied herself putting the final pieces of lattice into place on the *pastafrola* before standing back to admire her work.

"You know," Louise said. "I think this'd make a pretty great apology—if you were of that mind . . ."

This time Alicia couldn't hold herself back.

She turned on Louise with a biting fury.

"What makes you think that *I* should be the one apologising? What makes you think that *I'm* the one at fault?"

Louise held up her hands in a defensive posture. "Really," she said, "I wasn't saying that at all . . . *but*, you know, just remember what I said; about how women don't need to be damsels in distress. All they need is a plan, and they can accomplish anything."

Alicia allowed this advice to seep into her skull.

She really wasn't sure what to make of it.

And she couldn't shake the feeling that it was a touch condescending.

When she looked Louise back in the eye again, though, she saw that this was being sincerely offered. And that Alicia would be the asshole if she chose to throw it back in her face.

After giving the *pastafrola* a final look over, and correcting a less-than-perfectly placed piece of the lattice, she slipped it into the oven, along with the *pionono*, *alfajor* and *budín de pan*. The *tortas fritas*, which she had already fried, she slipped into the fridge to be reheated later on.

Finally, with no other cooking matters to distract her, Alicia looked Louise back in the eye, and said, "All right, what do you have in mind?"

———————

Alicia might've known from what she had said about women always needing a 'plan' that Louise wouldn't be naïve enough to come to the Orbital Café without one.

And it wasn't some half-assed, cobbled-together plan either.

Nope, this plan was fully realised.

Alicia caught onto that much when Louise led her outside, to a waiting PEAR.

Its visor already popped open.

As if they'd been suddenly transported back to a London street in nineteenth-century England, Louise guided Alicia into the PEAR, offering her a hand so that she might clamber in over the side.

When they took to the air, Alicia was in almost no doubt as to what their final destination would be. And, indeed, she wasn't wrong.

The Crescent Gardens swept out beneath the PEAR.

Already, Alicia could make out the pale white lights arranged among the greenery spread out below them. Once they'd alighted the PEAR and got into the Gardens themselves, Alicia realised that the source of each and every one of the lights was from a flame.

That they were candles.

As Alicia took in the setting, she caught sight of Wendy and then Njhay, the two of them apparently attempting to surreptitiously slip away from the scene before being spotted. Before they were held responsible for the work they'd clearly put into creating this *romantic* milieu.

Alicia glanced to Louise, only to find that she was gone.

When Alicia examined her surroundings, she realised that there was no sight of Wendy or Njhay now, either. As her eyes adapted to the near darkness of the Gardens, she saw there was a thick, woollen blanket spread out across one of the patches of grass.

A single candle sat on the blanket, holding back the surrounding darkness.

There was a bottle of wine, coupled with a pair of glasses, too.

Machiavelli would've been proud.

Because there didn't seem to be anything else more obvious to do, Alicia approached the blanket, then hovered over it a couple of moments before finally descending.

It was comfortable.

More comfortable than she'd imagined it would be.

The grass was springy beneath the blanket, and it was wonderful to be able to breathe in the scent of the flowers surrounding her. To feel as if the scent was cleansing her of the oil and baking fat which surely clung to her skin. It brought her back to those childhood days on the family farm; to those days when she'd had nothing to do except go exploring . . . back then it'd seemed as if she had the entire world to play in. Was that the attitude which'd brought her to the Moon?

As she knelt down on the blanket, she couldn't help but feel somewhat self-conscious. As if somewhere—*somehow*—someone was keeping their eye on her. Ever since Supervisor Nuha had informed her that she'd been *recorded* leaving the Dome without permission, she'd begun to feel as if her every action was being scrutinised. She supposed, now that she was sitting on two strikes, it was better for her to be cautious . . . even *paranoid* . . . although she had designed the words so that they might wind up Gofreddo, she knew that she had meant them.

After all, she *did* have a career to think about.

Dressed, like her, in his Celestial Stays overalls, Gofreddo emerged from seemingly nowhere.

His features seemed to slowly form from out of the gloom; his tufted, blond hair taking on a pale, almost ghostly quality, while his thick, muscular frame loomed larger and larger as he closed in.

Over his shoulder, she made out the PEAR taking to the skies, and leaving the Crescent Gardens behind. She couldn't help wondering if she didn't see Louise's face peering out through the visor. Perhaps she was waving to her as she left them to their business. One thing was for certain, though, the two of them were alone.

Alicia turned her attention upward, to Gofreddo.

She tried to read his expression in the obscurity.

It confused her slightly to see that he was gently smiling.

Her heart kicked on a few beats.

And her stomach crunched in on itself.

"*Buenas Noches,*" he said, that familiar smile—that impossibly warm, woozy tone—present in his voice.

"Evening," she said, and then, suddenly feeling self-conscious, and not entirely sure just what *she* wanted out of this exchange, she averted her gaze.

There was an uncomfortable few beats of silence before Gofreddo took it on himself to speak up.

"I am sorry," he said. "I am *very* sorry for not thinking things through." He paused for a second or so. "When I took you to see the Monument, I should have taken care to think about what the consequences might be—what might happen to *you* if something went wrong."

Alicia turned her gaze onto him.

Somehow it was difficult for her to think just *why* she'd ever been angry with him in the first place. It was difficult to stay angry with a man as dashing as he was. With such good manners. And with *those* slippery, innately *dangerous* blue eyes.

Eyes which reminded her of the searing skies back on the family farm; those skies which seemed to soar on into infinity. And there she went . . . losing herself all over again . . .

Thinking with her . . . well, she certainly wasn't thinking with her *head*.

She felt her chest tighten. She breathed in deeply, hoping that she might be able to mitigate the effect, but it only caused her to go light-headed . . . and light-headed *really* wasn't how she needed to be right now. She needed to have all her wits about her.

Otherwise she might make a *terrible* mistake.

It was as she was thinking through her response to Gofreddo that she noticed the nasal *whine* which was cutting through the air. That distinctive sound which was second nature anywhere on Earth, and which was certainly not absent here, on the Moon.

A delivery drone.

Gofreddo, too, seemed attracted by the sound.

It was a welcome distraction from an awkward moment as the two of them tilted their heads upward, to the sky above.

Alicia made out the drone soon enough. It wasn't all that difficult to spot given that it had a green starboard light and a red port light. At first, she believed that the drone was merely carrying on its flightpath *over* the Crescent Gardens.

But soon it occurred to her that it wasn't going *away* . . . it was coming *toward* them.

And it was descending.

Neither of them spoke as the drone's *whine* reduced to a low-level *buzz*.

As its quad-copter blades slowed as it approached the ground.

Soon enough, the drone landed beside them neatly in the grass.

Alicia immediately noticed the wicker picnic basket, replete with a red-and-white chequered table cloth lining the interior, and just peeping out from beneath the flap.

"What's this?" Gofreddo said, the amusement in his voice clear.

Alicia glanced back at him, doing her best to communicate that, really, she hadn't any better idea than he did. Saying that, though, she could tell from the smell. From that distinctive sweet odour of the guava jelly which she had used in the *pastafrola*.

Gofreddo glanced at her, apparently seeking her permission before opening the wicker basket.

"I had nothing to do with this," she finally had the sense to utter.

"All the same," he replied. "It smells *delicious*."

He peeled back the lid of the wicker picnic basket, and even Alicia had to admit that the sweet aromas were almost too much for her to bear. It was all she could manage to hold herself back from pawing through the contents of the basket and wedging cakes—and that *sweetness*—into her mouth. As she watched over his shoulder, she saw that, nestled within, and still steaming from the oven, there were all the treats she had prepared back in the Orbital Café kitchen.

How they'd got there was a mystery.

But one which she was glad to allow to exist for the time being.

The contents of the basket wasn't just the selection of treats which Alicia had been cooking, but slices of each one. A piece for both Alicia and Gofreddo to try.

Finally, after Gofreddo had withdrawn the entire contents of the picnic basket, and he had laid the treats out on the blanket beneath him, he turned to Alicia with wide eyes and said, "I don't think that I've seen such a feast as this since I was a little boy."

Although Alicia was wary he was on his best behaviour—that he was doing his level best to *flatter* her—she couldn't quite resist a quick blush.

Relieved of its cargo, the drone hummed back into life.

As with all drones, it looked somewhat unlikely to ever become airborne for several seconds before taking the final skip up into the air, levitating, and then finding its balance.

Just as quickly as it had come, the drone whined on off over the foliage of the Crescent Gardens. To wherever it was headed next. Something told Alicia that its next task wouldn't be as romantic.

The two of them had five different desserts to sample.

It was then that Alicia realised Gofreddo had turned to her.

And that he was bearing the slice of *pastafrola* in the palm of his hand.

"So," he said, "did you say this slice is mine or *yours?*"

Strangely, Alicia found herself forgetting very quickly about the two strikes she already had against her name by the time Gofreddo had thoroughly smothered her neck with kisses and was duly working his way further south. She could feel the slight stickiness which clung to his lips from the slice of *pastafrola* the two of them had shared. And she could smell the sweetness which emanated from his mouth each time he breathed out against her skin.

They hadn't managed to get as far as the *pionono*, the *tortas fritas*, the *alfajor*, let alone the *budín de pan*. And it was a welcome relief for Alicia to know that, back in the Orbital Café kitchen, the remnants of her baking would remain . . . so that tomorrow she could return to her cool-headed tasting and other analysis. But right now was hardly the time for a *cool* head.

As Gofreddo worked the zip of her overalls loose, she felt her heart beating harder and harder, seeming to claw its way—piece by piece—up her throat.

His hands were so gentle—so *careful*—that she almost didn't notice when she was rendered completely naked. He slipped her gently free of her overalls, and laid her down on the blanket.

She felt the warm, smooth material underneath her.

As she lay on her back, staring up at him, reflected against the candlelight of the Crescent Gardens, she couldn't quite comprehend that this was the same Gofreddo Zito who she'd read about in the media, what felt like every single day of her life.

Then again, she supposed that he *wasn't* the same Gofreddo Zito.

Because that Gofreddo Zito was merely an image.

A two-dimensional rendering created only as an efficient means of selling to the media.

Their bodies were the same.

But that was all.

And, goodness, was she *glad* for this body.

She surveyed his muscular form rising up above her.

He peeled himself free of his own overalls.

She took stock of his breathing.

Profound.

His blond hair was similar to that of a surfer; someone who spent all day out in the sun—someone who consistently washed themselves in the sea. There was that vital, natural element to him. That part which would never be tamed. But, then again, why *would* she ever want to tame it?

His arms appeared around her, thick and muscular, and *secure*.

She felt his body moving against hers.

It was all too much to take.

Her whole body went rigid.

It was then that she noticed something in his hand.

He held it delicately, as if afraid that it might break.

Or *crumble*.

When she finally caught a glimpse of his hand, she saw that it was a piece of *pionono*: the small, sweet pastry with a spiral shape. *Dulce de leche* in the centre. Already she could breathe in the sweetness emanating. She could see his gentle, loving smile as he laid it down on her bare breast.

His head ducked down, and she felt his tongue finding its way all over her skin. She felt his tongue finding the pastry, and seeming to become lost between her skin and the sweet texture.

The blood pumped to her temples.

And it seemed almost to steal her sense away.

When Gofreddo straightened his naked body up, and he leaned down over her, offering the remainder of the *pionono*, she lurched forward and snapped at it with her mouth.

He toyed with her, pulling it away.

But she was insistent.

She wouldn't allow a *man* to dominate her.

Acting swiftly, she reached out and grabbed hold of Gofreddo's wrist. She forced the *pionono*—enclosed by his fist—down into her mouth, taking the final bite.

She felt the dual sensation of Gofreddo's weight upon her, and the sweetness of the pastry slowly melting in her mouth.

She breathed quickly and unevenly. Unable to keep her wits about her.

But what use did she have for wits?

There was always tomorrow.

Tomorrow she could use her wits . . .

It was then that she felt herself losing her mind—losing all sense—to him.

And she allowed him to consume her.

ECLIPSE STRATEGY

*H*eat *seemed to billow forth* from every culinary orifice.

Sweet smells turned strangely sour in Alicia's nostrils.

Her throat tasted somehow bitter . . . and she *really* hoped it was because of stress, and not because of some sin she'd committed against Argentine cuisine.

The *clatter* of a saucepan brought her back to reality.

She gazed around.

The temporary dome's kitchen was more than sufficient, as she had already concluded when Gofreddo had brought her along on that sordid fact-finding mission. That 'mission' which'd almost cost Alicia her job. Or, at the very least, her command of the Orbital Café.

But that didn't mean she was suffering any less now.

It seemed as if *everything* was getting on top of her.

And because it felt as if the entire world was tumbling down about her ears, she tried to introduce a much-needed sense of perspective; if only for a moment. She had always had a habit for making a melodrama out of everything . . .

But, that said, how *could* things be worse?

Well, for one, she might be all the way back Earthside right now.

Jobless.

Prospectless.

Still, counting her blessings didn't improve her current dilemma all that much.

The dilemma which pertained to flavour.

She had somehow managed to convince herself that she'd made a *huge* error in choosing to use lemon, instead of lime, in the various treats she was preparing. It had been one of those impulse decisions which would simply *occur* from time to time; come at her like a bolt from the blue . . . and she was loath to go against her gut; especially when her trust in it could accurately have been described as *the* leading factor in her culinary success.

And now that she'd made the decision concrete, assigned it to the protocol which her staff were now following, she couldn't quite shake the idea from her mind that she'd made a *big* mistake.

She watched on as her kitchen staff went about their duties, going through all the steps which she had decided were to act as the blueprint.

But what if it went wrong?

What if Gofreddo's grandmother *hated* what Alicia rustled up?

Although Alicia had been to visit Argentina, she'd never been much outside of Buenos Aires. And, as her experience of globe-trotting had long ago taught her, to take any impressions about a country, a culture, simply from the capital city, was a grave mistake.

She glanced over Drake's shoulder as he worked to create the pastry lattice for the *pastafrola*. And she couldn't help but feel herself being swept back—back to that *wonderful* night a few days ago—in the Crescent Gardens. It took her a couple of moments to realise that Drake was staring at her, that he was talking about something or other.

Alicia snapped away from the memory of the passionate night spent in Gofreddo's embrace, on *that* blanket . . . with *those* flowers surrounding them.

"Boss? *Boss?*"

"Hmm?" Alicia said, turning her attention onto Drake.

Just like the other members of her staff she'd brought along to help out with the cooking, Drake looked somewhat rattled by the experience. Sure, they'd all signed on to work with the exclusive clientele of the Celestial Stays Dome, but it was another matter entirely to end up serving an *even more* exclusive element. Quite simply, the *crème de la crème*.

Or the *richest* of the *rich*.

"The temperature," Drake said, nodding toward the oven.

Millat and Stéphanie were nearby, preparing the *pionono* and the *tortas fritas*, respectively.

"What . . . what about the temperature?" Alicia finally managed to respond.

She was still having trouble ridding her mind of *those* infernal pecs—*goddammit!*

"In the instructions, according to the protocol, I downshift ten degrees for the final ten minutes of cooking time, but . . ." He trailed away briefly, as if he was loath to add anything more—finally he plucked up the courage, though. ". . . it looks to me as if it's still soft inside, as if it's gonna flop over itself. Why don't you take a look?"

Finally realising that Drake was referring to the *budín de pan* which'd gone into the oven a few moments previously, Alicia switched her mind to concentrate on the matter.

She dished out the instructions quickly, without a moment's hesitation.

And Drake nodded and went off to do her bidding.

The last item which they were preparing—the *alfajor*—Alicia had left to herself.

She had deliberately given herself arguably the easiest task.

Before Kyra had turned up in the Orbital Café kitchen to provide her with a better model for her management methods, Alicia would always assign herself the trickiest recipes to put together.

However, as she'd learned from Kyra, putting more pressure on her personal culinary performance would only mean that she was diluting the efficacy of her management methods.

Since Alicia had only to pop the *alfajores* into the oven and leave them, she hardly had anything else to do except dot the *i*'s and cross the *t*'s about the kitchen.

Thinking on Kyra, Alicia noted that she was standing in the doorway.

Since Kyra was only involved in a supervisory role—since she didn't seem to possess any *particular* culinary prowess of her own —she was really just here for moral support.

With a smile, Kyra approached, soon taking up what'd become a familiar place, standing just at Alicia's shoulder. Indeed, as Alicia looked over the kitchen, wondering what her next stroke might be, she felt Kyra's gentle touch. "I'll take it from here," she said. "You've been at this for *ages*."

Alicia shuddered beneath Kyra's touch. Not because her grip was too strong—and certainly not because she resented her presence here—but simply because she was tightly wound by the whole situation. It seemed as if so much as a falling speck of dust might set her off.

Although Kyra was surely telling the truth—Alicia had arrived here, to the temporary dome kitchens first thing this morning—she couldn't quite bring herself to accept that she now had to let things go. That she had to pass the proceedings into someone else's hands. Right on the cusp of rejecting Kyra's suggestion, Alicia found herself on the end of another woman's stare.

Louise.

She, too, appeared out of seemingly nowhere.

Without a word to Alicia, Louise took hold of her shoulder and eased her away from the kitchen. Although Alicia knew that it was strictly against what the two women were attempting to achieve between them, she couldn't help but snatch a glance back over her shoulder; a final look at the kitchen—at the *state of play*, as it stood.

And as it slipped out of sight, she couldn't help wondering to herself if she hadn't witnessed Millat splodging on *far* too much *dulce de leche* while he rolled a *pionono*; or if she couldn't smell the thick, unmistakeable scent of Stéphanie burning the *tortas fritas*; if she had *really* seen Drake drop one of the fledgling lattices for the *pastafrola* on the floor, only to retrieve it, give it a quick blow to rid it of any visible dust before replacing it upon the pastry.

"My, oh my," Louise said, almost casually. "You really *are* tense." She gave a shake of her head. "It seems like *you* could do with a massage."

"Yeah, well," Alicia replied, "some of us have work to do."

Louise removed her hold on Alicia temporarily, and then gave her a wide-eyed expression. "And so *feisty* too." Her expression was transformed by a toothy grin. "*Passionate*."

As Louise guided Alicia through the temporary dome—and *away* from the kitchen-slash-disaster area—she couldn't help but take in the décor . . . how the place had been done up for the celebration. Louise had personally picked out the flowers to decorate the temporary dome, and she had tended to go with reds and pinks, which, Alicia supposed, were meant to compliment how the Moon would appear back on Earth—how it would appear in the sky as what was commonly known as a 'blood Moon'.

Alicia noted Njhay skulking about on the periphery, wearing, like the rest of them had been instructed, formal dress instead of the usual, day-to-day overalls. He wore a tuxedo tonight, the option which all of the male guests attending were expected to settle on.

Only now did Alicia turn her attention properly onto Louise. She realised that she was wearing a prim, light-pink dress which ended just above the thigh. As they passed by a mirror, Alicia got a quick chance to see her own current appearance.

She had gone with a black cocktail dress tonight—*jet-black*.

Only now did she realise that it seemed a somewhat *funereal* choice.

If she hadn't thought it consciously then something had almost certainly been gnawing away at the back of her mind, edging her toward the idea that this *was* a sombre event.

Noticing several wrinkles in the front of her dress from where she had had the apron tied on in the kitchen, Alicia smoothed them out quickly. At some point in the process of her extraction from the kitchen, Kyra and Louise had somehow conspired to remove the apron over Alicia's head.

They moved away from the mirror.

In the main viewing area of the dome, Alicia couldn't help noting the platform which'd been erected, replete with chairs for the assembled guests to get the best view possible of the eclipse when it finally occurred. Although she knew very little about science—and even *less* about astronomy—the way she understood the eclipse was that it would be similar to a solar eclipse back on Earth . . . only, instead of the Moon blocking out the sun, it would be the Earth.

Louise stuck her finger into her earpiece, apparently communicating with the Link. Alicia knew that the Link's influence had been extended specially to this temporary dome for the duration of the event . . . just as it hadn't been when Alicia and Gofreddo had come here for their 'visit'.

She turned into Alicia.

Smiled.

It was one of those smiles which sent a tingle down Alicia's spine.

"They're here," Louise simply said.

And Alicia was so tightly wound—her mind had been so rattled by all the work she'd put into the preparations for the baked treats —that she had the temerity to ask, "*Who?*"

Louise had the good sense not to answer.

She only reached down and clasped Alicia's hand with her own.

Alicia really had no idea what to expect of herself as Louise escorted her into the lobby of the dome. Up ahead, she could already make out the landing pad, and the Shuttle as it descended. She made out Gofreddo sat in the pilot's chair. She lost herself in that *handsome* face of his; that look of total concentration as he brought the Shuttle, along with its precious cargo, down on the landing pad.

Her heart beat harder.

And her blood ran cool.

She wondered if this was all still a fling...

The first person off the Shuttle was Lan Niu—the member of the Security Division.

Unlike the rest of the employees already present at the dome, she wasn't wearing any sort of formal wear. Just like every day, she had on her black overalls, and, Alicia couldn't help noticing, the blaster pistol holstered at her thigh.

She felt a twinge of guilt, almost as if she was *physically* reaching out for the pistol; making the unwise decision of attempting to disarm Lan.

Next off the Shuttle was Supervisor Mackenzie Angliss.

The two of them exchanged a pleasant, professional smile, although Alicia couldn't help but wonder just what might be going through Mackenzie's mind.

She knew that if there was any impediment to Alicia's advancement through the Celestial Stays hierarchy then it would come from her.

Tonight Alicia knew that Mackenzie would be watching her like a hawk, seeing whether there was any reason for taking further action against her.

Now, or in the future.

Thinking about it, Alicia realised that her whole career could depend on how this evening went. It seemed almost as if Mackenzie was in disguise to be wearing that flowing, deep-purple gown which brought attention to her sleek, shimmering—*fiery*—red hair. Almost as if she was far too stunning—too *radiant*—to be here for any other reason than leisure.

But, as Alicia well knew about career women such as Mackenzie—such as *herself*—there was never a way of completely switching off...

Supervisor Habiba Nuha got off the Shuttle behind Mackenzie Angliss.

Alicia felt her heart sink down to her stomach.

She knew that Habiba, Supervisor of Catering, was here to look over her own end of the proceedings—the savoury portion of the alimentation—but Alicia couldn't quite shake the feeling that she was also here to keep an eye on her. Almost like a backup measure if anything should become of Kyra. Between the two of them, they could keep a careful eye on Alicia.

Habiba wore an elegant, beige ceremonial gown with silver and gold threading which Alicia supposed to be traditional to her country of origin: the Ivory Coast.

When she caught Habiba's eye, she gave her a smile.

But Alicia just felt an emptiness hollow her chest.

Habiba, Mackenzie and Lan all stood in a row at the ramp which jutted out beneath the Shuttle. It was almost as if they were forming a welcoming committee for a foreign dignitary.

Then again Alicia supposed that Costantino Zito probably *did* outrank the dignitaries of several smaller-sized countries.

Louise tugged Alicia by the elbow, bringing them into line.

Alicia observed the wheelchair emerge along the ramp. Paula Zito, wore a floaty, flowery dress which showed off a pair of well-formed legs. Although Alicia hadn't had a chance to consider Paula's figure before, she did now. In her time—in her *youth*—Alicia couldn't help thinking that she would have been quite the fox . . .

Wendy appeared behind Paula, pushing her chair.

And then there was Gofreddo.

Alicia's heart near enough stopped all over again.

Despite having seen the pictures—*countless pictures*—of Gofreddo Zito appearing at varying functions and occasions in a tuxedo, and other manners of formal dress, it was one thing to see those glossy photos and quite another to see it in real life.

She could tell that he'd taken some effort to tame his tufty blond hair.

To some extent, he had succeeded.

As he emerged from the Shuttle, he beamed that winning *Zito* smile at all those waiting.

When Alicia cast a glance over Habiba and Mackenzie, she saw that even Lan was smiling away at him; apparently the Ice Queen of the Security Division was unable to resist his charms . . . well, she'd certainly 'overlooked' his own unauthorised egress and ingress to the Dome, there had to be *some* secret.

As Wendy walked Paula Zito's wheelchair past Alicia and Louise, Alicia was certain that Gofreddo, too, would just keep on walking by. That he would go through to the viewing area in the company of his grandmother.

However, seemingly out of nowhere, he glanced around.

Caught Alicia's eye.

Her heart bounced up to the back of her mouth.

He locked her with his stare.

That *sky-blue* stare.

And he held out his hand.

Alicia must've been resisting forward motion, because it was only with Louise's heavy prompting—a solid *poke* in her lower back—that eventually caused her to accept his offer.

She felt his warm, strong grip.

She could tell that, ahead of the evening, he had spent some time getting a manicure. His hands themselves, too, were unnaturally well-moisturised, although she could still feel the underlying cracked skin . . . the evidence of hard work back on his childhood *finca?*

Just as Alicia herself had put the work in on her childhood farm.

Alicia felt everyone's eyes on her as she walked beside Gofreddo.

She almost tripped a couple of times when she realised that her bosses Habiba Nuha and Mackenzie Angliss were seeing all this.

What would they make of it?

What conclusions *could* they draw?

And yet Alicia pushed away all those concerns. She pushed away the concerns which surrounded the kitchen; all of that baking which was being carried out under her guidance, but without her supervision. She simply *let it go* . . .

When Alicia returned to the viewing area, she noted that circular tables had been assembled on the platform. And that each one had a formal, white table cloth dangling down over it. She took in the candles, too. That really completed the effect. Made it seem as if it *truly was* romantic.

Once she'd sat down, she turned her attention onto the kitchen doors, and was on the brink of rising up out of her seat when she felt a familiar touch on her shoulder.

It was Louise, again.

This time she was in the arms of Njhay.

There was no need for words.

Louise only gave Alicia a no-nonsense shake of the head.

And, somehow, it seemed to do the trick.

Sat at their table was Wendy, Paula, Gofreddo and herself.

Alicia had panicked to begin with, believing somehow that she might end up seated with Mackenzie and Habiba. And she really hadn't the will to explain her relationship with Gofreddo right now. It was one thing too many for her to handle.

As Gofreddo conversed with his grandmother in their native Spanish, Alicia busied herself with taking in the details of the dome. She watched on as the other guests arrived, all of them in formal clothing: tuxedos and cocktail dresses.

Alicia was glad that she hadn't arrived too elegantly.

In her book, the only thing worse than underdressing was *overdressing*.

In all, there were about a dozen tables all laid out; seven or eight people to each table. A fairly sizeable amount of people for the occasion. She thought about all the bedrooms which were located throughout here and couldn't help wondering why Celestial Stays didn't think about making this a permanent site.

It was only when the band struck up that Alicia noticed them at all.

She shifted a glance to the string quartet; to the two violins, the viola and the cello.

All of them women.

All of them in formal attire.

Alicia couldn't quite shake the feeling that she was back on Earth.

That she'd returned to prom night.

"Alicia?"

She turned her attention back to the table, taking in Gofreddo sat there, and beaming at her. It was only then she noticed that there was a waiter patiently standing at their table, clearly anticipating her order. After a brief scrabble for a menu, Gofreddo informed her that it was a set option and that she was to choose between having her eggs scrambled or poached.

She went with poached, which seemed to satisfy the waiter.

Once the waiter had disappeared from the table, she looked over at Gofreddo and asked him what it was the eggs would accompany.

"Salmon," he replied, succinctly, his lips full and . . . well, *kissable*.

" 'Salmon' " Alicia repeated to herself, feeling nothing but an airhead.

As Gofreddo continued his discussion with his grandmother in Spanish, Alicia couldn't help but notice Wendy shifting glances in her direction.

Finally, with a cautionary look to Gofreddo and his grandmother—the two of them still immersed in discussion—Wendy said, in a restrained voice, almost a whisper, "You know, I'm so happy about the two of you." She flashed her eyebrows. "From all the conversations I've had with Costantino, Gofreddo's had a hard time finding someone."

" 'Someone' ?" Alicia replied, still a little thunderstruck that they were even having this conversation, although what she had expected, she couldn't rightly say.

Wendy nodded. "Well who *doesn't* know about his profile, hmm? But"—she cast another glance in Gofreddo and his grandmother's direction—"what you've got to understand is that all the glitz and glamour, all of those famous meanderings of his, it's all just a façade; just a sleight of hand . . . a way of throwing attention away from himself."

It was somewhat surreal to be having this conversation at the same table Gofreddo sat at, although, she had to admit, he seemed more than occupied with the conversation with his grandmother.

Hypnotised, even.

Alicia frowned. "Isn't all of that stuff"—she paused, tried to think of another word to use next, and failed—"his *reputation,* him?"

Wendy shook her head. And then looked off ruefully in Gofreddo's direction. "No, it's really not—not deep down. Not from what I've heard about him. Not from what I've experienced *first-hand.*"

From that point, the conversation slipped into silence.

What did Alicia have to say?

How well did she *really* know Gofreddo?

. . . One thing was for certain, they'd never got around to discussing their plans, their dreams . . . their *future.*

"Yum, yum," Wendy said.

Alicia glanced up, saw that the waiters were bringing out the first course.

And despite the gorgeous, buttery smells—despite the odour of salt and pepper and *olive oil* rippling through the air—she didn't feel a smudge of hunger.

23

EVENT IMPLEMENTATION

*T*he *starter* turned out to be salmon and eggs, as had been hinted at by the waiter taking their orders. One of the most difficult things about having dedicated her life to flavour—to *pleasure*—was that she'd grown accustomed to taking her time, to turning a mouthful into a seven-course meal. The modest plate of salmon and poached eggs seemed nothing short of a feast.

And then there was the anticipation.

The worry about how her Argentine specialities would turn out.

Alicia somehow managed to get the salmon and poached eggs down, but the next course—a basil-and-pesto lasagne—proved a far more difficult proposition, and she could only finish about a quarter of it. As she pushed it about her plate, she was all too aware of Gofreddo's grandmother staring daggers at her.

Alicia was certain, as always seemed to be the way with mothers—*goodness*, hadn't it been the way with her own?—that wasting food was only marginally better than killing in cold blood.

But, all the same, she said nothing.

She and Gofreddo continued their conversation, leaving Wendy and Alicia to their awkward silence. If it hadn't been for the string quartet sawing away in the background, Alicia had little idea just *how* she might survive the evening.

As Alicia had coordinated with Habiba, the waiters next brought out plates of either the *pionono*, the *pastafrola* or the *budín de pan* . . . the *tortas fritas* and the *alfajor* would be served with coffee or tea once dessert was over and done with.

Alicia remained almost paralysed as she found herself staring down at the perfect slice of *pastafrola* sitting on the plate before her. Her whole body went rigid, as if she was afraid to take so much as a bite. When she glanced across the table, she saw that Gofreddo had gone for the *pionono*, while Wendy had elected the *budín de pan*.

Gofreddo's grandmother had chosen the same as Alicia.

The *pastafrola*.

For a long while, Alicia was caught between panic and delight.

She wondered if she'd done something right, or if she'd done something terribly wrong, judging by the wide smile which split Paula Zito's lips.

When Alicia turned her attention back to her own pudding, she noticed that the vanilla ice cream which'd been served with the *pastafrola* had already melted into a sticky puddle. She ducked down, as if sitting an exam, and pushed herself through to devouring the entire dessert.

It was all over before Alicia could really collect her thoughts.

She glanced up, to the table, and then to the rest of the room.

Empty plates.

Some of them looking as if they'd been licked clean.

It allowed Alicia to relax slightly.

But not all the way.

Already, she made out the waiters meandering between tables, taking orders for coffee or tea, and informing them of the choice of cakes and biscuits which would be brought out by way of accompaniment. Alicia couldn't help noticing Paula Zito's pouting expression as she took in the options as they were offered to her by the waiter.

As she often would do, peeping out from behind the kitchen door at her customers, she tried to read anything at all . . . *approval, disapproval . . . indifference?*

Again, it all happened so quickly.

The coffee and tea were served.

The tray containing the *tortas fritas* and *alfajor*es was delivered.

In a kind of daze, Alicia went for tea over coffee.

She really could do with something soothing—something to calm her nerves—rather than something which'd get her all wound up. All over again.

Once more, she watched on as Gofreddo helped his grand-mother to the sugary treats.

And, again, she wasn't any the wiser just how Paula Zito felt about the food.

Once the plates had been cleared away, refills of tea and coffee were offered to the guests. Alicia also noticed that there were a couple of—*not-so-subtle*—requests for alcohol of different sorts.

She overheard one party requesting champagne, while another, older gentleman, was asking after some whisky to wash his dinner down with.

Despite the fact that alcohol was *officially* prohibited on the Moon, as with all prohibitive measures, it'd only served to make things worse; to give the guests an even greater thirst than they might already have had. And far be it from Celestial Stays to have a guest go home short of being completely *content* in every conceivable manner.

Indeed, as Alicia allowed herself to lean back fractionally in her chair, she noted the waiters surreptitiously bringing out flasks which might've contained just about anything . . . but which, Alicia knew from experience, contained that which had been requested.

Her spy operations were curtailed when she felt someone tap her on the shoulder.

When she turned, she saw that it was Kyra.

She was dressed in a flowing sari with embroidered designs of suns and Moons and stars.

Although she was certain she'd been wearing it earlier, Alicia hadn't noticed.

The item of clothing reminded Alicia of the oven gloves she'd unceremoniously tossed out once it'd become obvious that they weren't fit for purpose any longer.

"How was it?" Kyra said, smiling all over.

Although Alicia *wanted* to assure her that everything had gone off without a hitch—that everything had been *just fine*—she couldn't quite bring herself to make her answer as glowing as the quality of the baking had surely deserved.

"Great, thanks," she managed to get out.

Sure enough, she noted the slight lessening of the intensity of Kyra's grin.

Alicia had never been a good liar.

"*Terrific*," Kyra said, covering up her obvious disappointment as she retreated from the table, and headed back to the kitchen.

Although feeling as if things couldn't have gone any worse, her attention was distracted by the sudden burst of a voice above the room; above the sound of the string quartet.

After the first few syllables, the string quartet ground to an abrupt halt.

Alicia turned her attention down onto the area before them.

And she took in Mackenzie.

As if she hadn't had the time to appreciate Mackenzie's dress before, she had another opportunity now. Really, it was *beyond* stunning. She felt a knot form in her stomach and a strange almost jealous yearning or realisation that she would never, ever—no matter how hard she tried—look as elegant as Supervisor Mackenzie Angliss did right then.

"Ladies and gentlemen," Mackenzie said, her voice throaty, always on the cusp of being *vicious* . . . all those qualities which Alicia wished *her* voice might possess.

"First of all, I would like to thank all of the kind attentions and efforts put in place by the staff for tonight's meal."

Here the guests broke out in applause.

From the table where Alicia had heard the guests ordering champagne, there was stamping too.

"It's my duty to inform you," Mackenzie continued, "that the eclipse will take place in the next ten minutes. You are advised to take up a position where you will be able to best view the phenomenon."

Here Mackenzie glanced about the room—a gesture which, Alicia was certain, was a product of a lifetime spent undertaking public-speaking roles.

If only *Alicia* had that confidence.

That *self-assurance* . . . then she would be the unmistakable next Supervisor of Catering.

"Once again, Celestial Stays would like to thank you for choosing the *Moon* as your destination. *The Destination of a Lifetime.*"

Funnily enough, hearing Celestial Stays's well-worn tagline spilling out from between Mackenzie's lips seemed the most natural thing in the whole world.

With that done, and another smattering of applause among the guests, there was the discordant symphony of chairs scraping against the floor as people all moved toward the viewing platform; everybody wanting to get a good look at the eclipse as it happened.

The moment when the Earth blocked out the Sun.

To say it was a once-in-a-lifetime event seemed almost an understatement.

Because who could afford a trip to the Moon a *second* time?

On instinct, Alicia looked to Wendy, then to Gofreddo and his grandmother, seeing that they were already stirring from their places. Getting ready to take in the sight as the Earth slipped in front of the sun, blocking it out.

Despite hardly having eaten a bite of dinner, Alicia felt heavy as she rocked herself up onto her feet. She accompanied the others over to the glass and stood up there, to look out across the lunar plains. Of course, as had been the whole point in locating the temporary dome here, the Lunar One Monument dominated the landscape.

At the present moment, it was glimmering in the sunrays.

That rendering of the cylindrical, doomed spaceship.

The one which'd accompanied Alicia's childhood.

Just as it had for surely *every* child growing up on Earth.

The ever-present caution of the stakes mankind played with while they pushed back frontiers.

It happened so quickly that Alicia hardly noticed.

First there was the gentle, unmistakable feel of Gofreddo's finger up against her hand.

And then she felt his fingers entwine about hers.

Alicia felt hesitant.

She was still raging with anxiety, with apprehension—and subsequent *disappointment*—which'd accompanied the evening.

When he squeezed her hand, she looked across at him, and saw that he was pensive, staring out through the glass. To the lunar plains beyond.

She wondered if he was thinking about his grandfather—the man he'd never known.

The man who'd been a hero.

One of those hero *explorers*.

As the Earth dipped across the sun, rendering the eclipse complete, the whole dome descended into an uneasy silence. Light was replaced by shadow. By almost complete darkness. Nobody had thought to turn on any of the lights within the dome.

And Alicia was glad.

She wanted to feel the night.

She wished to feel its gentle nibble against her skin.

It was then that someone—*Mackenzie?*—gave the order for the string quartet to strike back up.

Alicia felt Gofreddo clench her hand all the tighter.

It sent a throb through her heart.

The whole world seemed to converge on Alicia during that moment.

When Gofreddo spoke to her, she was slightly surprised that his lips were so close to her ears. That she could feel his warming breath up against her neck. "Shall we dance?"

In all her years of world travel, after all the languages she had picked up, Alicia had somehow never got around to learning how to dance. It was one of the few survival skills which had evaded her. But if there was one thing which she *had* learned during her travels, it was that whenever she found herself in a situation where she simply *had* to dance then she was always better off following the cue of the other dancer.

That was the trick to being a bad dancer.

She supposed what Gofreddo was dancing to be a waltz. She was fairly certain that they were following the steps which she'd seen in countless films and various TV shows. To begin with, as they danced, Alicia could do nothing except look down, wary that she might tread on Gofreddo's—very nicely polished—dress shoes.

That was one thing which all men certainly *didn't* appreciate.

A heel to the middle of the foot.

"It's okay," Gofreddo said, his voice calm and smooth.

She glanced up at him. Near enough stumbled. But he caught her before she had the chance to build up momentum; to surely end up smashing her nose against the dance floor.

Yeah, that really *would* have been the way to cap a humiliating evening.

Finally, though, Alicia managed to find the rhythm of Gofreddo's steps. She caught the rhythm to such an extent that she no longer had to shift glances at his feet to make sure she wasn't about to do him any lasting damage.

Despite finding her dancing shoes—against all odds—she couldn't help but let out a brisk sigh.

Apparently not missing so much as a detail—and certainly not missing so much as a single *step*—Gofreddo said, "What's wrong? What's the matter?"

Alicia remembered where she was.

She recalled the occasion.

What it meant to Gofreddo.

What it meant to his grandmother.

Just who did she think she was to be making this all about her?

What *right* did she have?

But, then again, Gofreddo *had* asked.

Shaking her head, she turned her eyes onto Gofreddo's sky-blues.

"It's just that I feel I let you down."

Here Gofreddo halted their dance momentarily.

He leaned back from her, still holding her firmly. " 'Let me down' ?" he asked. "*How?*"

Alicia allowed a pause, and then said, "You know, with the treats I prepared—in honour of your grandmother. They were . . . they were—"

"*Delicious*," Gofreddo finished for her.

"Right," Alicia replied, "I . . . I'm sure they were—but it's just that, I'm worried, you know . . ."

" 'Worried' about what?"

She glanced about the dome, her gaze resting for several seconds on Gofreddo's grandmother, where she sat in her wheelchair, hands clasped in her lap, almost in meditation.

She shifted her attention back to Gofreddo. "I wanted to do something *special*. Something that would be remembered always."

This time Gofreddo's motions were quick.

He was almost forceful with his gestures.

His eyes had a sharpness to them when he looked on her now.

"And why would you think you failed at that task?"

"Because," Alicia began. "I . . . I don't know." She shook her head, and forced a smile onto her lips. "I'm sorry," she continued, "I feel like I'm being totally pathetic. Forget I said anything."

To begin with, Alicia was certain that Gofreddo was going to try and 'make things right'; that he was going to attempt to *fix*

198

things all over again. That *male* habit which simply drove her crazy.

But, after staring at her longingly for what felt like a good portion of eternity, he continued to guide her about the dance floor . . .

Now having found her rhythm, she followed Gofreddo's steps effortlessly.

She couldn't help haphazardly wondering what he might be like when he had a *good* dance partner. She wondered what his tango might be like . . . that was what they danced in Argentina, wasn't it? Perhaps, once she'd mastered the waltz, she could have a go at the tango.

It must have been a little over an hour when Mackenzie called every soul in the room together once again. So that they might witness the end of the eclipse.

Already Alicia could make out that a kind of dawn was sweeping the lunar plains, as the Sun appeared from behind the Earth. She felt Gofreddo's soothing hand on her back, just below her shoulder blades. It felt as if he had all the strength in the world.

That it all laid *coiled* within him.

Ready to burst free at any moment.

As the Sun emerged from behind the Earth, glimmering and strong, and blazing its light all across the lunar plains—causing the Lunar One Monument to glitter—Gofreddo turned into Alicia and dropped his voice down low; a husky whisper.

"My grandmother would like to speak with you." He paused for an impossibly long moment. "Before she goes," he added.

Alicia looked around, finally locating Paula Zito in her wheelchair, with Wendy standing behind like some perennial guard . . . for some reason it put Alicia in mind of those Pharaohs who took their most faithful warriors with them into the afterlife.

She took a deep breath and wondered what the worst thing that could happen was.

Gofreddo's grandmother didn't *look* like she would bite.

But who was Alicia to say?

Clinging to the crook of Gofreddo's arm, she felt her heart pulsing in her mouth. She could feel the blood running about her body, chilling her all over with apprehension. It was funny to think that a frail old lady—so close to death—had the ability to frighten her so senseless.

They got about a dozen or so paces from Paula Zito before Gofreddo released her. As Alicia glanced up, to Paula herself, she saw that Wendy had slipped away surreptitiously.

That the two of them would *truly* be alone.

Another deep breath later, and Alicia was by Paula Zito's side.

"Uh, *Buenas noches, señora*," she got out, raking her brain for the Spanish knowledge she hadn't needed to draw on in years.

"*Buenas noches, cariño*," Paula Zito replied.

"Is it okay for me to speak in English?"

Paula gave a curt nod.

And a smile.

This warmed Alicia all over.

It felt almost as if her every worry had been in vain; that she'd been making mountains out of molehills. *All over again.*

Alicia searched briefly for something to say, and then managed, "Have you enjoyed the evening so far?"

Paula Zito smiled widely. "It has been *most* wonderful."

This warmed Alicia further still.

What had she been worried about?

"It's really, uh, a pleasure to meet you," Alicia said.

"Really, *cariño*, the pleasure is *all* mine."

Alicia felt somewhat stunned by this statement.

One thing she'd learned during her travels throughout Latin America was that people tended to be more forthright when expressing their thoughts.

Their *emotions*.

She regained her footing.

"I'm pleased to hear it," Alicia answered, finally, and then decided now was the time to sound Paula out . . . although she knew it was a little thing—something which really shouldn't have mattered—if she didn't ask then it would bother her *forever*.

Cooking was really *that* important to her life.

"Please, Señora Costantino, would you tell me what you thought about the food I prepared this evening. The Argentine cuisine?"

Paula Zito paused for a long time, her lips pert. The skin around her eyes wrinkled as she turned the matter over. Finally, as if she'd given the question a great deal of mental bandwidth, she turned her full attention back onto Alicia.

"You used *lemons* instead of limes, correct?"

Alicia felt herself blush.

Sure, before she had been paranoid about preparing national cuisine which she wasn't familiar with; now, though, it was clear that she was dealing with an *expert*.

She nodded in reply to Paula Zito's question.

"Hmm," Paula Zito replied, actually bringing her hand up to cup her chin. "Yes, I thought as much, I could *taste* it . . ."

Despite her frail tone of voice, and her obviously ailing appearance, Alicia couldn't help but sound somewhat insistent. "And?" she said, raising her eyebrows.

Paula Zito smiled again.

She brought her wrinkled-up fingers to her pert lips, gave them a brief kiss, and then fluttered her fingers free. *"Magnifico,"* she said, with an even wider smile.

Alicia felt as if she could die happy.

She glanced around, seeing that Gofreddo still lurked on the periphery, no doubt readying himself to dive into the conversation if Alicia got herself ensnared in any serious trouble. But, somehow, Alicia thought she and Paula Zito would get along just fine from now on.

"Come closer."

Alicia turned her attention back to Paula Zito.

Saw her staring up at her.

There was a watery quality to her eyes, as if she was on the brink of tears.

Noticing Paula's outstretched fingers, Alicia took her hand in her own.

Her bones reminded her of a bird's nest: those intricate, delicate constructions she would often find littering the long grasses following a storm . . . eggs long gone, and Mother Bird flown away.

When Alicia looked into Paula's eyes properly now, she saw that she had the same irises as Gofreddo. That searing, endless sky-blue colour.

"I am so glad," Paula said. "So glad that Gofreddo has found someone like you—someone to make him feel calm; to give him a *purpose.*"

Alicia wasn't completely sure about what Paula said here.

Her heart skipped a couple of beats.

She wondered if she should think to correct Paula, to tell her that, at least as far as *she* was concerned, they'd only just begun to feel one another out. It would be a large leap of logic to conclude that they had any sort of long-term future ahead.

Although, Alicia had to admit, the idea intrigued her.

Greatly.

Paula grinned more widely than she had throughout the entirety of their conversation. "And to have found one so *talented*, too..."

It was there that Alicia caught Paula's eye and the silent message seemed to pass between them.

Somehow Paula read it loud and clear.

She squeezed Alicia's hand all the tighter.

"It might seem like nothing now," Paula said, "but I have great many years of experience, I know these things. I know what to look for. I have been through all of it for myself. And I know that you and Gofreddo are destined to remain together." The strength of her smile lessened by a few degrees. "He might seem somewhat confused—*you yourself* are no doubt somewhat confused—but together the two of you shall work out what your life's purpose shall be. Trust that. Trust in your love."

It was that last word—*love*—which continued to ring about Alicia's skull as she left the viewing section of the dome behind; as she trekked her way down the corridor to the room she had been assigned for the evening.

As she left the string quartet—still sawing away—and the various dancing guests, she wondered what that word even meant. And if she truly felt it for Gofreddo.

Still thinking it through, she slipped in beneath the bedsheets and allowed herself to drift away into a well-deserved, and ultimately *satisfied*, sleep.

Alicia woke in the darkness.

Of course it was dark.

Before getting into bed, she had ordered the blackout blinds down so the sunrays wouldn't interfere with her sleep. It was strange to think about inhabiting the Moon. Normally, when she was back in the Basements, there was no need to give windows so much as a second thought.

She could make out a figure moving through the gloom.

And she had only to breathe in to know just who it was.

Gofreddo.

How he'd got into her room—how he had known which room had been assigned her—was a mystery. Then again, she wouldn't have been at all surprised to learn that certain portions of information were far more easily obtained by a Costantino than by a Brennan.

She supposed he believed her to be sleeping.

And she watched him through the veil of darkness.

She observed him slipping free of his tuxedo jacket, and then undoing the hand-knotted bowtie.

Soon enough, he stood only in his dress trousers, with his bare midriff exposed. She supposed that light from somewhere—*the corridor?*—managed to seep into the room. She could make out the glint reflecting off his tightly muscled six-pack.

Still half lost in the world of her dreams, and feeling dozy, she noted him gently slide off his trousers too; hang them up off the back of a chair.

And then he approached the bed.

He took great care not to disturb her, gradually lowering himself down and then slipping in beneath the bedsheets. Lying alongside her.

She felt his warmth.

And she felt his easy respiration.

When she cast a glance across his face, she saw that his eyes remained half open, and that his lips were slightly parted. Acting on impulse, she reached out to him.

When her fingertips made contact with his hard skin, it felt as if she was using all the force of a jackhammer to smash through the tranquillity of this moment. She expected him to flinch. To be rendered surprised that she was awake at all. But, instead, after feeling her touch, he gently turned his head to her. And a slight smile teased at his lips.

"My grandmother has passed away," he said.

Alicia felt a knot form in her throat.

But she swallowed it back down.

Forced herself not to cry.

How many times had she cried for her own grandmother?

How many tears had she shed over the years at her inability to be there right until the end?

Somehow, following the conversation she and Paula Zito had had, she felt almost as if she had made peace with some other-worldly force. As if she had—*somehow*—brought the cosmos back into some kind of balance.

Her *own* personal cosmos, that was ...

"I'm sorry," Alicia said, because she could think of nothing else.

Gofreddo reached out and slid his fingers through her hair.

She felt his large, muscular fingers slip past her ears.

It brought another warm wave up through her chest.

She eased her foot along Gofreddo's calf, feeling the more and more familiar sensation of his body lying beside her own.

He leaned into her.

Planted a kiss on her lips.

Then he drew back.

Smiling widely.

Tears were there, too.

But they weren't tears of grief.

They were tears of *joy*.

"It was perfect," he said, his voice a whisper, even though there was no one around to overhear him. "Just *perfect*." He leaned into her and kissed her again—this time harder. *Longer*. He drew back. "You were wonderful. My *abuelita*, she said that she'd never eaten such delicious treats since she was a little girl—the idea to use the lemons." He shook his head. "She said that, in the village where she grew up, the baker would always use lemons. My *abuelita* herself would use lemons. She had grown to believe that it was a secret which only she knew of . . ."

Alicia felt the breath stripped from her lungs.

She was rendered unable to speak for several seconds.

And then she forced herself to reply.

"It was just a feeling," she said. "Just an *impulse*."

Gofreddo smacked his lips in delight, smiled, and then leaned in to kiss her again.

Before she had quite caught her breath—before she had quite allowed herself an, apparently, well-deserved pat on the back—she felt Gofreddo kneeling, as if to get up.

He was gentle as he lowered himself onto her.

Alicia reached up and ran her hands through his hair.

Without really thinking about it—without *needing* to think about it—she uttered the word which Paula Zito had used to describe their relationship.

"I *love* you," Alicia said.

24

BURIAL RITES

*W*hen *Alicia woke* the next morning, she was alone. She blinked the sleep from her eyes. Her neural implant buzzed away in her frontal lobe. The Link informed her that there was a message waiting. It was from Gofreddo.

Feeling somewhat dizzy from the events of the night before, she ordered the message to be read out through her earpiece:

Alicia,

This morning is the funeral for my grandmother. It would be wonderful if you would be able to attend. I am currently having meetings with those responsible, working out the arrangements. I shall be by to check on you later.

Yo a tí, te amo. — I love you too.

Gofreddo

Alicia blinked away her sleep. She hadn't felt so drowsy in a long while. Perhaps that was the effect dinner and dancing had on her. Although she would've much rather remained beneath the bedsheets until the end of time, she forced herself to shuck them off.

They landed in a pile on the floor, at her feet.

When she glanced up, she saw that Gofreddo's tuxedo suit continued to hang off the back of the chair, and that his shoes had been left behind also. She wondered what sort of attire he had settled on for these 'meetings'.

The Link informed her that there was someone at the door, and she was about halfway to answering when she caught sight of herself in a full-length mirror.

And realised she was stark naked.

Thinking quickly, she tore one of the provided dressing gowns off its hanger and threw it about her shoulders. She tied it tight about her waist and then answered the door.

Standing in the doorway was Kyra.

She beamed back at Alicia, now wearing her standard-issue overalls in place of the sari she'd worn the night before.

Because thinking of words was apparently harder than simply *acting* this morning, Alicia lurched forward and grappled Kyra in her embrace, pulling her into her chest and giving her a long squeeze. Once Alicia had got through with this impromptu hug, Kyra was blushing a touch.

"I just wanted to say," Kyra was able to get out, finally, "that I've had all the equipment packed up—I took care of all the cleaning, well . . ." Her voice trailed off here. ". . . I *supervised* the kitchen staff's efforts at cleaning." She smiled more broadly. "Didn't want to get my party frock all soiled, did I?"

"Thank you," Alicia said, now finding her voice. "Thank you for *everything*."

Kyra gave Alicia a mock salute. "Don't mention it—and now I'd better shove off; we don't want anything untoward to become of the Orbital Café kitchen, now, do we?"

"Absolutely not."

Kyra had already turned side on to leave when she appeared to recall something and turned back around. "Ah," she said. "There was one thing."

"Hmm?" Alicia said, still sufficiently stuck in a daze that she really couldn't have cared less about any matters concerning her duties . . . not *right* now . . .

"I spoke with Mackenzie Angliss."

Despite her relaxed state of mind and body, Alicia felt her stomach clench.

"She's decided," Kyra continued, "that I'm no longer required—that you should be entrusted to the management of the Orbital Café without any further interference."

"Oh," Alicia said, feeling strangely light-headed . . . and not a little conflicted. "Is that right?"

Kyra gave a nod. "I'll look over the Orbital Café this afternoon —make sure that everything's ship shape. From the way I understand it, you'll have your hands full today." One corner of her mouth slipped back in a smile of sympathy. She reached out and squeezed Alicia's shoulder. "I hope everything goes well," she said.

And then she trod off down the hallway.

Alicia remained standing in the doorway until, across the hall, she heard another door sliding open. Realising that she wasn't exactly in a state of dress which would facilitate positive interaction with strangers, she quickly ducked back into her room.

And fixed her ideas—firmly—on taking a steaming-hot shower.

When Alicia had got through with her shower, and she'd wrapped herself in one of the impossibly fluffy towels provided in the room, she realised that a fresh, long-skirted dress had been left out for her. Unlike the dress she'd worn the night before, it wasn't black.

She supposed this wasn't going to be a typical funeral.

The dress was a light-pink shade and, as soon as Alicia slipped it on over her head, she saw how it brought out the peach colour in her cheeks. Whoever had had the job of picking her dress, they had certainly had Alicia's appearance well and truly in mind.

Once the Link advised Alicia that there was someone else at the door, she was all ready to go.

When she answered, she found that it was Louise and Njhay standing there. Like Alicia, neither of the two of them was wearing black. Louise had gone with a cornflower-blue dress while Njhay wore a pale-grey suit with a tie to match Louise's dress.

Louise met Alicia's eye. "Gofreddo asked the two of us along, for moral support."

Alicia was confused for a moment or so. "But he barely knows you."

Louise smirked. "No," she said, "moral support for *you*."

"Oh," Alicia replied, suddenly feeling like a ditz.

Together, they proceeded through the dome; moving through the viewing area which'd been vacated of the circular tables from the night before. If Alicia could say one thing for Celestial Stays, then it was that they were extremely efficient.

On the ride in the PEAR to the Lunar One Monument—the final resting place of the victims of the crash, and where Paula Zito would be buried—Louise explained to Alicia about what'd occurred the night before. Whether or not Gofreddo had told her himself, or if it was merely gossip, Alicia didn't think to ask. She told Alicia that, as had been previously arranged, a doctor had been present with what Louise phrased a 'pain-control kit' . . . the upshot of this 'pain-control kit' was that, when Paula requested so, she would be allowed to slip away.

To leave this reality.

And move onto the next.

She had chosen last night to do it.

Alicia thought back to Gofreddo; thought about his reaction.

Perhaps that was the reason why he hadn't been too shaken up by his grandmother's death. She had been allowed to go out on her own terms—no pain, no anxiety—and safe in the knowledge that when she did embark on her eternal sleep she would do it beside the one she had loved throughout her life. Her own personal hero.

The Lunar One Monument had been specially buffed up for the occasion.

Alicia took in the various markers used for the graves.

She read the plaques.

Of course, accordingly with various members of the crew's religious beliefs—or the beliefs of their families—some of these plaques had nothing but lunar dust beneath them. With the bodies either buried elsewhere or otherwise dealt with. Costantino Senior, though, was buried beneath his assigned plaque. And Alicia's eyes immediately shifted to the dug-out, rectangular pit beside it.

Then to the rosewood coffin, ready to be interred.

There weren't more than a dozen people present at the service.

And there were no chairs.

She shifted her gaze across the faces—all of them dour and reflective in one way or another. She picked out Gofreddo before too long. For some reason, she had always imagined that someone like him—someone of his *profile*—would wear lunky sunglasses on an occasion such as this one. The purpose was surely to maintain some modicum of privacy from the press's all-seeing lens.

But here, on the Moon, there was hardly any reason for him to hide at all.

Throughout the ceremony, Alicia remained still.

She kept her hands down at her sides.

And she felt her pulse gradually ticking along.

Almost as if her whole body stood in reverence.

When they placed Paula Zito in the ground, a complete silence fell over the assembled crowd. And Alicia watched on as the Sun dipped down beneath the lunar horizon, and then she switched her attention upward, to the Earth, still on the rise.

She wondered what it'd been like for Paula Zito. Every time she had turned her attention up to the night-time sky had she been able to see the Moon; or could she never get beyond the fact that she was *always* staring at her husband's final resting place?

The end of his tragic voyage . . .

There was no clearly demarcated ending to the ceremony. In that way, it was much like the other, terrestrial, funerals which Alicia had attended. Everybody just seemed to drift away from the Lunar One Monument, in the direction of the Shuttle waiting to take them all back to the Celestial Stays Dome.

While the others all boarded the Shuttle, Alicia hung back,

unwilling to leave Gofreddo behind here; all alone with his grand-mother's grave. With everybody else buckling up in the Shuttle and readying to leave, she felt a gentle touch on her shoulder. When she turned, she saw that it was Louise. "Come on," she said, her voice smooth and sweet. "He asked for some time alone—he wanted some time to be here, at the memorial, without anyone else around."

Alicia hung back for another few moments before realising the truth in what Louise said.

If Alicia had been in Gofreddo's situation, wouldn't she have wanted the same thing?

Some time to let the facts settle?

Coiling her arm more tightly about Alicia's shoulder now, Louise added, "They'll be by to pick him up in an hour or so. You can speak with him when you're back at the Dome."

Alicia finally relented, deciding that she had no choice but to leave him behind . . . although it seemed so strange; after last night, after their intimacy.

After what Paula Zito had said to her.

When Alicia took her seat on the Shuttle, bringing her chest straps across, and the shoulder straps down, she couldn't help but get a final look at Gofreddo and the Lunar One Monument.

She stared long and hard, seeing Gofreddo's back to her.

She squinted to be sure of what she saw . . . Was he? . . . Yes, he was sticking his finger into his earpiece . . . Contacting the Link? . . . Most likely speaking with his father . . .

With Costantino Zito.

He would want to know what'd gone on.

How it had all *panned out* . . .

"Hey?"

Alicia turned in her seat, to Louise sitting beside her.

When she brought Louise back into focus, she saw what she held in her palm.

A pair of *alfajores*, wrapped in a white, paper napkin.

In the sterile, disinfectant-smelling air of the Shuttle, the sweet odour of the biscuits seemed almost like an elixir. Alicia lost herself to the sensation for several seconds. And she felt herself being whipped back—just for the fraction of a moment—to Earth . . . and to all its culinary joys.

All of the joys which she'd brought to the Moon.

"White chocolate or dark chocolate?" Louise said, grinning.

Alicia forced herself to smile. It made her feel better. "Decisions, decisions," she said, and then flipped a final glance out of the window at Gofreddo before turning her attention onto the sugary snacks.

25

MEDIA BRIEFING

offreddo felt as if every part of him had frozen solid.

His torso.

His legs.

His arms.

His blood.

. . . His *heart*.

He vaguely watched as the lights of the Shuttle disappeared over the horizon, headed back to the Celestial Stays Dome. He really *was* all alone now . . . and yet, not *quite*.

He had forgotten to switch his earpiece to Standby before the commencement of the ceremony.

When the Link—via his earpiece—had informed him that he had a new message waiting, he had shut it off. Once his grandmother had been committed to the lunar dunes, to rest forevermore beside his grandfather, a whole manner of things had been on his mind.

But the first one which apparently needed dealing with was the waiting message.

It was out of curiosity more than anything else, and if the sender had been anyone other than Costantino Zito—*his father*—then he would've been sure to stash the message away for perusal at some as-yet unspecified date. However it *had* been from his father.

And its contents had nearly been enough to turn his stomach.

When he'd first opened it, he'd expected that his father would be requesting his personal account of the ceremony. He might even have been so organised as to wish to check in with Gofreddo for certain important documentation which accompanied his grandmother's burial.

But, no.

The message he'd received was as follows:

Hijo,

It is with a terribly heavy heart that I write to you, today of all days, with some extremely unpleasant news.

Down here, on Earth, the media have learned of your grandmother's burial on the Moon. The editor concerned was good enough to get in touch with me, and the story shall not go to press until this evening. I asked for that much, so that you should hear it from me first.

I am sure you understand what this implies; that you can no longer afford to place your trust in those around you—those on the lunar surface. The leak has come from someone up there. Someone close to you.

Once the story goes to press, we shall have a chance to discuss the future—to see what the next step shall be.

Be careful.

Papá

Gofreddo stood and looked out over the lunar plains for so long.

Many—*many*—things passed through his mind.

He tried to work out the *who* and the *why* and the *when*.

But the answer was clear all along. It was more of a cautionary tale, really.

His comeuppance.

This was what he got for trusting *Alicia Brennan*.

26

CONSPIRATORIAL PROGRAMMING

*T*he *buttery steam* poured out from beneath the lid of the saucepan. Alicia caught it at the back of her throat. It seemed like almost nothing said 'home' like the warming, sweet smells of cooking.

As she laid the lid down on the counter, she listened to the butter crackle away within the saucepan as it melted. She gave a contented sigh.

Soon things would be back to normal . . . whatever 'normal' was on the Moon.

True to say that she and Gofreddo hadn't been in touch over the course of the past day, but she was mature enough to realise that, more than anything else, he needed space.

And she was willing to allow him that space.

If what Paula Zito had told her was true—that she *really was* special to Gofreddo—then she could trust that he would return to her once he had dealt with his emotional wounds. That was one thing she had picked up about men. When they were hurting over something it was best just to leave them to it. Let them pick up the pieces all on their own.

She threw herself into her cooking, finding a renewed vigour to be back in the Orbital Café kitchens with her staff vying to do her bidding.

Although she wasn't about to thank anybody for Mackenzie Angliss having Kyra placed on her case—making sure she wouldn't flip out over anything—she had to admit that it'd done everything to revolutionise her management style.

Speaking of 'management style', she had sent her staff home early again tonight, giving them a well-earned, long Friday afternoon. When Alicia had stopped to think about it, she decided that her staff had really done her tremendously proud with their baking for Paula Zito's final night. Ever since then, she'd been thinking of ways in which she could repay them, and she hoped to come up with some solution in the next week or so.

As she poured the liquefied, boiling butter out into a bowl and set it on the side, she heard footsteps behind her.

Her heart fluttered up to her throat.

Because she knew just who it would be.

Gofreddo.

She allowed herself to draw the moment out; to give her heart the chance to throb away.

These were the moments that she needed to cherish.

These were the times that she had to *remember.*

If things really did work out, it would be funny to think about telling her grandchildren—*grandchildren?!*—about her and Gofreddo's escapades on the Moon.

Finally, with the buttery scent still hanging in the air, she turned around.

But it wasn't Gofreddo.

It was Wendy.

Wendy Flowme.

"Wendy?" Alicia said, smiling. "What're you doing here?"

Wendy remained straight-faced. "I've come here to bring you a message."

" 'A message' ?" Alicia said, the smile slipping from her lips. "What about? Who from?"

"*Gofreddo*," she said.

Alicia screwed up her brow, unable to understand. "I . . . What do you mean?"

"He has something to say. But he doesn't want anything to do with you. He can't *afford* to have anything else to do with you."

Suddenly catching onto what was going on, Alicia bunched her fingers into fists down at her side. "Listen," she said, "if this is some sort of joke then I'm not laughing."

Wendy remained stern. "It is not a joke, Alicia." She paused. "I'm sorry."

Alicia scanned Wendy for any sign that she was enjoying herself.

But all she could interpret was hard-headed stoicism.

Could this be for real?

"Why—*why* won't he speak to me?"

"You know the reason," Wendy said. "You know what the problem is."

"No, no I *don't*."

Wendy shrugged.

Alicia remained focussed. "Look," she said. "If Gofreddo is indeed 'unable' to speak with me, then I have to admit I have no idea why he chose to send you here. Why didn't he come himself?"

"We ran the decision by Mackenzie Angliss. She told me to

come along. It wouldn't have been appropriate to expose Gofreddo any longer."

This whole conversation was really starting to make her head hurt. "And what *is* the 'situation'?"

"The stories," Wendy finally said, cryptically.

Alicia shook her head. "The 'stories'?"

"In the media. The ones which *you* leaked out about his grandmother—about Paula Zito—about her plan to live out her last moments on the lunar surface before being buried at her husband's side."

Alicia sensed that Wendy was becoming increasingly uncomfortable now.

She wondered if she'd anticipated spending this long around her.

From the whole context—from the whole act—it seemed as if she had come here with the intention of getting out as soon as possible.

"For a start," Alicia said, "I don't know *anything* about any stories."

She was surprised at how she managed to keep her tone so civil.

"What about the pictures?"

"What *'pictures'*?"

"The ones taken at the funeral."

"I . . ."

Wendy took a step toward her. "You really *are* a mad bitch, Alicia. I never would've *imagined* that you would have something like this in you; that you would be able to profit from someone else's misery." She shook her head. "I thought you were better than that. I thought I *knew* you better than that . . . that you wouldn't sell out the Zitos."

Through everything—through the anger and bemusement—Alicia managed to crack through and ask the calm question. "What was the message?" she said. "What was the *exact* message Gofreddo wanted to send me?"

"That you're to enjoy your life," Wendy replied, and then, almost spitting, "That you're to enjoy your *career.*"

And, with that, Wendy stormed out.

Alicia stood still, feeling her heart thumping at the back of her mouth.

Unsure what she should do now.

Was there anything she could do now?

Alicia finished up cooking as quickly as she could, not wanting to dither longer than necessary. She wanted to clear up whatever confusion had developed. She needed to get answers. Any future relationship she was to have with Gofreddo relied on it. Because there seemed no other obvious place to go, she headed to the Basements. She recalled Gofreddo's apartment location from the time she'd been there before, and wondered at her wisdom when she stood on the doorstep.

What if he had a security detail?

What if he had taken *extreme* measures to keep her from seeing him?

All of those details seemed irrelevant for the time being since he wouldn't come to the door. The Link informed her that there was no one at home. And she decided to believe the Link . . . *for now.*

Thinking on what Wendy had said, she decided to make her next stop Mackenzie Angliss's office in the Lunar Grand. As she rose up the elevator, staring out at the Celestial Stays complex which surrounded the hotel, she couldn't help wondering if Paula Zito had quite simply been mistaken. If she had seen something which hadn't been there at all—what if the 'love' she'd witnessed between the two of them turned out to be nothing more than a wrongly interpreted glance?

What if both she and Gofreddo had read one another wrong.

What if they really did have no future?

Alicia pushed away the doubts, telling herself to buck up for the looming meeting with Mackenzie. One thing was for certain, if she went into the meeting without every single one of her wits about her then Mackenzie would chew her up and spit her out.

Even though Alicia hadn't done anything wrong.

Even though she couldn't *think* of anything she'd done wrong.

She'd believed that he'd trusted her.

That she'd got into his 'inner circle'.

But, clearly, she'd been mistaken.

Mackenzie had her back to Alicia when she arrived to her office. She also had her finger stuck into her ear as she issued orders, checking for information, through the Link, via her neural implant.

Alicia was patient, knowing that she needed to keep her calm if she was to get her answers. When Mackenzie finally did turn around, she gave Alicia a once-over glance, and then gestured for her to take a seat in front of her desk.

Alicia had no intention of sitting.

"What's going on?" Alicia said.

"I could ask you the same question."

Alicia breathed in deeply. "Please," she said. "This *thing* . . . whatever's gone on with the media—you have to understand that I've had nothing to do with it . . . nothing *at all*."

Mackenzie studied Alicia very closely. "You do realise what the seriousness of this matter would be if Gofreddo Zito was still a guest at Celestial Stays, and not—*technically*—an employee?"

"Why's he only 'technically' an employee?"

"Well, because he doesn't draw a salary. Doesn't need one. I suppose that leads him to being far more like a *slave* than anything else, doesn't it?"

Alicia waited out a beat knowing instinctively that Mackenzie would speak up; that she would fill the silence. Sure enough, she did.

"According to the terms of the contract you signed, you are *prohibited* from going public about any of our guests or employees." She gave a shake of her head. "It'd be grounds for *immediate* dismissal."

It was a strange feeling, to have that skittering sensation pass up her spine, and to know, at the same time, she had done nothing at all wrong.

"But he's *not* an employee or a guest," Alicia said.

Mackenzie flashed her eyebrows. "And, believe me, I've been working on a solution all morning to try and tie off *that* discrepancy." She sighed, then propped herself up against the edge of her desk. She dropped her head and stared at her hands as they supported her. "I did wonder whether I could dismiss you based on Paula Zito being implicated in the media reports." She glanced back up. "But Legal inform me that it won't fly . . ." She rolled her eyes. "I've never had a lot of truck with Legal."

"So," Alicia said, "where does that leave me?"

"Where does it leave you?" Mackenzie asked. "Where do you *think* it leaves you—it leaves you *still bloody here* . . . but without many friends."

A long silence filled the office.

It was unlike Mackenzie to speak so frankly—to fail to check her emotion.

Alicia knew that she had to put her point across now.

"I'm innocent," she said. "I did nothing at all."

Mackenzie levered herself up away from her desk. "I'm sorry, Alicia, but I've seen the evidence, and it's irrefutable. If it'd just been the media stories, without the photos at the funeral, then maybe . . . *maybe* . . ." Again, she shook her head. "Anyway, I wouldn't worry *too much* about it; you're not going to get fired or anything."

Without thinking, Alicia responded, half to herself, "But I might lose the man I *love* over it . . ."

If Mackenzie did hear her then she didn't respond.

But, then again, Mackenzie had never had much 'truck' with sentimentality.

"I want to speak to him," Alicia said. "Can you tell me where he is?"

Mackenzie glanced up.

Met Alicia's eyes.

Another long silence draped over the two of them.

"You're telling the truth, aren't you?" Mackenzie said. "I mean, you sound *honest* about what you're saying." She shrugged her shoulders, breathing in deep, anticipating, no doubt, an extremely profound sigh. "What'd I know about people, though; they never cease to amaze me." She breathed out the sigh, met Alicia's eye once again. "They never cease to *disappoint* me."

"Just tell me how I can speak with him," Alicia said. "That's all I'm asking."

Mackenzie remained very still for the longest time, and then said, "I promised him that I'd cut off all contact—prevent you from getting any more dough to sell. He was pretty sure about that."

"Please, Mackenzie."

Another few seconds passed.

Then Mackenzie dipped her head.

"I'll send the info across the Link . . . you can do as you wish." She paused a final time, and then added, "I should warn you that he's pretty pissed."

Feeling a touch giddy now at the prospect of being able to speak with Gofreddo face to face, Alicia almost chuckled her reply. "It's okay," she said, "I can manage 'pretty pissed' just fine."

It turned out that Gofreddo was in the Shuttle Hangar.

If he'd been angling for a top-secret retreat then there was little doubt that he'd failed completely on that account. She had hardly any trouble at all in tracking him; finding him lying on one of those skateboard-type devices most often used by the garden-variety car mechanic down on Earth.

As she eyed him through the glass of the Shuttle Hangar, she found herself contending with another obstacle. Lan Niu of the Security Division.

Niu cut an imposing figure, what with her angled haircut and the sheer, jet-black overalls.

"Access denied," she said, speaking firmly, unambiguously.

"I have permission from Angliss—Mackenzie Angliss, Supervisor of Human Resources."

Lan pouted, shrugged. "Doesn't matter to me—I take my orders from Security. Not Human Resources."

Alicia eyed Lan closely. "Please," she said. "This is important. I promise I'll be quick. I just need a word, that's all."

But Lan remained where she stood. "Sorry," she said.

And almost sounded apologetic about it.

Alicia looked over the hangar, wondering if there was another way in. She couldn't see one, and, from the apparently strict—albeit *unseen*—security controls which were engaged about its circumference, she wouldn't have been surprised to discover that there was only a single way in.

And Lan was standing in the way.

Alicia opened her mouth to try pleading some more, and then, with Lan apparently occupied by the unspoken words lying on her lips, she acted.

She rushed Lan.

Not really knowing what she was doing, Alicia went at her with her elbow.

A sort of modified shoulder-charge.

She pumped her legs as hard as she could.

Right at the moment that she drew the closest to her target—*to Lan*—she witnessed her eyes widening in shock. And in that moment, Alicia knew she had her beaten.

The next sound was a cry as Lan tumbled backward and dropped to the ground.

Then there was the damp *thud* as she struck.

Alicia didn't stop to see what the damage was—to see if Lan might be in need of medical attention. Later on, it would disturb her that she could be so cold-blooded, but, at that moment, she knew only Gofreddo mattered.

Once inside the hangar, she noted everyone turned to look at her. She supposed she'd caused something of a kerfuffle outside, what with her forced entry and everything.

Gofreddo was the last one to turn in Alicia's direction.

His eyes widened and his mouth gaped.

Alicia's heart beat hard in her mouth.

She wondered what she was going to do now.

But, thankfully, her legs seemed to take over.

With a strange confidence she'd never thought she possessed, she strode past the gawping onlookers—the other Shuttle pilots, among them Patrick Fourie—and made her way up to Gofreddo. She half expected him to back away, to try and make some kind of an escape. But she knew Gofreddo Zito—or, at least, she knew the reputation he had built up for himself in the media.

It wouldn't be like him to back down from a challenge.

From a *confrontation*.

"Can we talk?" Alicia said.

Gofreddo glanced about. His gaze finally settled on the doorway to the hangar, just above Alicia. Before Alicia had the chance to turn and look, she heard Lan Niu's voice.

"Get down—*down on the ground!*"

There was no need for Alicia to turn.

She knew Lan had her in the blaster pistol's sights.

If she so wished, she could smudge Alicia out right now.

But Alicia held herself very still.

She met with Gofreddo's blinding blue eyes.

And waited.

Finally, she got out the word.

"Please."

27

VERBAL-MENTAL INTERACTION

ofreddo held Alicia in his gaze.

Despite everything—despite the circumstances—he had been a coward.

He could admit that to himself if he couldn't quite manage to say as much out loud.

How'd it got into his head to have Wendy Flowme do his dirty work for him?

When did it *ever* seem like that would come off?

He turned his attention onto Alicia again.

Took in those tangerine eyes of hers.

There was a *yearning* there, he could tell.

But it didn't make everything all right.

He had already discussed the situation with his father and, between the two of them, they had decided that the best course of action would be for Gofreddo to return Earthside. Just as Alicia had eluded to earlier on in their relationship—before she had *betrayed* him—his father would help him to find something mean-ingful; something which would allow Gofreddo to fill his other-wise empty days. If they'd settled on one thing between them following their respective lunar escapades, it was that Gofreddo had had *more* than enough time dedicated to being a young libertine.

Now he needed to make a man of himself.

Just as his father had done.

Whatever he had shared with Alicia, it was done with.

She had betrayed him.

Been unable to resist the money.

And he had trusted her . . . he had told her that he *loved* her . . .

He tried to figure it out now.

Did he still . . . Did he still feel something for her?

It was impossible to say for certain.

To an extent, everything seemed like noise.

These past few days had felt like an entire lifetime.

A lifetime passing him by.

If he didn't take his chance now, he might miss out entirely . . .

He felt Alicia reach out to him, her fingertips brushing his skin. He felt her warmth transferring into his body. He felt his heart give a slight *skip*. He seemed a touch out of breath.

A bout of giddiness struck him.

When he snapped back to reality—*to the present moment*—he took stock of the member of the Security Division assigned to him, on his father's insistence.

She stood with her blaster pistol pointed directly at Alicia.

Ready to fire.

Another shout.

Gofreddo knew this was the time.

This was *his* time.

Without another conscious thought, he dived in front of Alicia.

He was aware of an impossibly bright flash.

A percussive *thump*.

And then darkness.

28

VITAL SIGNS

licia felt as if she was sweating all over. Despite the air temperature, resting at an even twenty-five degrees, according to the Link, she felt as if she'd somehow ended up in the middle of the Sun. She breathed in the stilted, disinfected air of the Infirmary and tried to get her head around what'd just happened; the situation which'd just played out in the Shuttle Hangar.

It made her twitch—her muscles tense—just to think of it.

She recalled Lan Niu calling out for her to hit the ground.

To give herself up.

Alicia knew Lan had pointed the blaster at her.

And Alicia, in that moment, she realised, had been prepared to die.

She hadn't moved a muscle, even when she sensed Lan firing on her.

... And then ... well, it'd been a blur ... *too fast* to track.

Gofreddo had hurled himself.

He ... over her ... and then ...

"Alicia?"

She snapped her neck upward. She was blinded temporarily by the bright corridor lights of the Infirmary. At first, the figure standing before her was only an odd, hardly comprehensible shape.

Soon enough, though, her brain filled in the missing pieces.

The blond hair.

The blue eyes.

The fixed, intense look of concern.

Louise Williams.

Louise.

Her closest friend.

Before Alicia could react at all, Louise had thrown her arms about her, and tugged Alicia's face down into her chest. As Alicia felt herself pressed into Louise's soft breast, she listened to the calming voice close by her ear . . . Louise trying to get through to her.

"I came as soon as I heard," she said. "I'm so sorry—so sorry that this happened."

Alicia's heart thumped gently in her ears.

She was still in shock.

She knew that.

On a *logical* level she knew that.

And yet she didn't seem able to communicate the fact to her body.

She was numb.

When she breathed in, she was certain she could still sense that brutal, burning scent of the laser cutting through the air. Followed by the sharp, coppery smell of blood.

The sinking of her heart.

How her whole body had seized up.

For the smallest of seconds, she recalled meeting Lan Niu's eye.

Looking over the sight of the laser blaster.

Right into her eye.

They could only have stared at one another for moments.

Moments before all the shouting.

All the action.

The call for medical attention.

And, in the panic, Alicia had been allowed to tag along.

To ride here—*to the Infirmary*—with Gofreddo.

Alicia pushed the recollections away from her immediate thoughts.

She wanted to rid herself of the smells.

Those *smells.*

She hoped and prayed they wouldn't be her last sensory memory of Gofreddo.

It seemed too sombre to think of Gofreddo in terms of 'memory' at all.

She turned her attention to Louise again.

Took in her zesty, lemony smell.

And that made Alicia think of Paula Zito.

Of her remarks about the treats she'd prepared.

Would she ever be able to feel *normal* again?

"How's she holding up?"

Alicia felt Louise retreat from her.

When Louise had stepped out of the way, Alicia caught sight of Mackenzie Angliss.

Her heart sank.

She'd hoped that it would be Supervisor Habiba.

Somehow, Alicia felt that she would've been more sympathetic to the situation.

. . . But then did Alicia have any right—*any right at all*—to sympathy?

She had caused this, after all.

She was the reason why Gofreddo was fighting for his life.

If only she'd gone about the situation more logically—with a *clearer* head.

Then again, what was clear-headed about falling in love on the Moon?

Mackenzie's red hair was drawn back into an efficient ponytail, and Alicia was glad to see that her expression was as understanding—as *womanly*—as she could recall.

"You poor dear," Mackenzie said, her voice almost a *purr.* "I'm so sorry that this happened." She wrinkled her brow. "I've spoken with Security, about certain protocols, about certain *permissions* that never should've been granted. There's no way that someone should be stalking about the Dome with a lethal weapon." She breathed a harsh sigh, then slipped Louise a sidelong glance. "That said, it seems this goes further up than any of us—further than the Security Supervisor, even." She turned her attention back to Alicia, stone-faced. "I guess that when a Zito's involved, rules and regulations get broken faster than unsecured glassware in a Shuttle." Here she gave the slightest of smiles. "Especially, from what I've heard, one which happens to be piloted by Gofreddo Zito . . ."

It was so weird.

Just to hear his name spoken out loud made it seem like he was dead.

But he wasn't.

Not yet.

The doctor had told Alicia to wait here, out in the corridor, until they had further news.

She had insisted that he make her a promise to give her any

information on Gofreddo's vital status as soon as he had it. She wouldn't be left in the dark.

Not now.

"Mackenzie," Louise said.

It surprised Alicia.

She had almost forgotten Louise was there at all.

She turned to her, seeing that she wore an uneasy expression.

Before Louise spoke again, she exchanged another quick glance with Alicia. The focus of her attention returned to Mackenzie. "There's something I need to tell you."

Mackenzie pouted. "Can it wait?" she said. "This isn't really the time."

"It's about Alicia," Louise said, now sounding unsure, almost *embarrassed.* "It's about what's happened to her—about these *media* reports that've come out on Earth."

It was as if Louise had just fired off a firework at a funeral.

Alicia was all too conscious of both Mackenzie and Louise turning their burning gaze onto her; seeming almost to trap her there . . .

"It's okay," Alicia said. "You can talk." She gave a shrug, and half a smile. "I guess I'd like to get what's *actually* happened cleared up just as much as anybody else."

Louise gave Alicia a gentle, sympathetic smile, and then she turned her attention back to Mackenzie. "Before I say anything, I want you to understand that I couldn't speak about this earlier . . . the, uh, *circumstances* in which I found out about it meant that I was sworn to secrecy."

"And what 'circumstances' are these?" Mackenzie cut in with a tone so brutal that it was almost out of place to hear it in the context of the sombre atmosphere of the Infirmary corridor.

"During the Alex-Barn thing," Louise said.

Despite everything—despite the perilous situation Gofreddo found himself in—Alicia recalled the whole episode with Louise's ex-lover, Alex Barn; how he had gone several shades of crazy out in the Lunar Caverns . . . and how Louise had ended up confronting him.

Alicia could only thank her lucky stars that she hadn't found herself in a similar situation with Julius Denisov . . . yet.

There was something about the Celestial Stays Dome which bred a special sort of cabin fever; something about the *air* here which seemed to set people off.

"Remember when we were searching for Alex?" Louise continued. "When nobody could track him down? Well, I got a tip from someone." She paused for moment, coloured slightly, and then went on, "This *person*, I mean."

"Which person?" Mackenzie asked, now sounding angrier than ever.

It being a known fact that Alicia and Louise were best friends, Alicia could understand Mackenzie being wary to any 'foul play' that might be cranking into place.

That Louise might be attempting to save Alicia's skin.

Only to throw someone else to the sharks.

Alicia noted Mackenzie's suspicious glance pass over her.

She was searching for hesitation.

For any sign of improvisation.

"It was Kyra," Louise blurted out, finally.

Alicia's chest tightened.

She felt a throb of blood at her temples.

A migraine coming on . . . it wouldn't be any wonder.

"She was studying," Louise continued, "in the Armstrong Archive, when she came across Alex Barn there, she saw him studying the plans for the Lunar Caverns . . . that was how she knew where he'd got to—that was why I could track him down there."

Alicia felt the air between them become more taut.

More than anything, she wanted to slip Mackenzie a glance, to see what she might be making of these revelations, but she was afraid.

"When I pressed her—asked her what she was *doing* in the Archive herself—she swore me to secrecy; told me that she was doing some research on behalf of a media outlet." Here Louise took a profound breath—breathed it out. "She told me that she's a journalist, working undercover."

Silence pressed down on them now.

And then, as if by some mystical cue, Alicia realised that she could hear the steady *slap* of footsteps growing louder down the corridor.

They all turned their attention away from the current conversation.

And to the approaching doctor.

Alicia had to stretch just about every muscle in her legs to keep up with the doctor's heels. As she felt herself being catapulted along, she could hear Louise and Mackenzie continuing to converse between themselves. It seemed to happen in a kind of dreamy fog.

Although the conversation took place—and Alicia was *aware* of the conversation—it was as if it merely *floated* through her mind. In one ear and out the other.

" . . . I never assigned her, of course," Mackenzie said, her voice hurried, matching their quick pace down the corridor.

Alicia kept her eyes fixed on the doctor's heels.

Determined not to stumble or trip.

He had informed them that Gofreddo was conscious.

And that he was asking after Alicia.

Mackenzie and Louise were coming along on the ride, as much out of shock as anything else.

They had simply been swept along on the urgent wave.

"... The picnic at the Crescent Gardens," Louise said, "when I arranged for Alicia to meet with Gofreddo ... that was my fault ... I never thought ... never *stopped* to think ... I had Kyra prepare the picnic ... asked her to send the treats along using one of the kitchen drones ..."

Mackenzie interrupted her as they drew close to a pair of double doors which abruptly slid out of their way. "She must have known already," she said. "About the relationship ... Why else would she have thought to position herself within the Orbital Café kitchen?"

Losing her concentration for a second, Alicia stumbled.

But the doctor was alert.

He caught her before she could crash into the wall.

Trembling now, as she caught her balance and returned to her feet, she wondered dizzily if the doctor was used to coping with disoriented hangers-on; people who could quite easily have an accident themselves.

After another few steps, the doctor came to a halt.

He glanced back over them.

His eyes appeared almost to bulge from their sockets.

Alicia couldn't help wondering just how often they were called upon to perform life-saving surgery ... she didn't suppose that blaster wounds were all that common an ailment beneath the Celestial Stays Dome.

"All right," the doctor said, red-faced, and if not accustomed to performing surgery like this, then certainly not used to having to run as he had just done. "He's conscious but somewhat frail. Under sedation." He reached up and adjusted his glasses.

Alicia hadn't even noticed he'd been *wearing* glasses until right now.

"He might be a touch dopey, just to let you know, but he's come through the surgery fine."

Alicia still wasn't quite able to handle what he was saying.

She thought that she got the point, but she couldn't be sure.

"He's . . . okay?" Alicia asked.

The doctor seemed awfully reluctant to commit all of a sudden.

He reached up and adjusted his glasses again.

"He needs rest," the doctor said. "But I see no harm in you having five minutes with him."

Alicia glanced to Mackenzie and Louise, gave them a nod, and then she ventured into the room which the doctor indicated.

Like any other room in the Infirmary, there were no windows which looked out onto the Celestial Stays Dome. Only the dynamic wallpaper, currently showing off a fanned-out, hospital-green design. Alicia fixed her stare on Gofreddo.

It wasn't too tricky.

He dominated the room, lying slumped up in bed.

She saw that he had a couple of intravenous tubes running into his left wrist.

Slowly—and 'dopily', as the doctor had alluded to—Gofreddo turned his head in Alicia's direction. His eyes, usually so sharp, seemed to be squashed beneath a gloopy swamp.

She crouched down beside his bed, reached out and touched

him on the underside of his arm. Her heart throbbed harder in her throat. From what she could make out of him—his exposed bare chest—he had some cotton-white dressing wrapped about him.

Where Lan had shot him.

A touch of anger passed through Alicia's blood.

This was her fault.

All her fault.

"I'm sorry," she finally got out. "Sorry for *everything*."

When she took in Gofreddo's face, she saw that he was smiling lightly at her. He flexed his arm, and, seeing the tubes in his arm bending, Alicia told him to stay put.

Instead, he used his free right arm to reach out and stroke her cheek.

When he spoke his voice was husky, and weak.

It was a side of him which Alicia had never previously experienced.

"I am sorry, too. I should have known you had nothing to do with this."

Alicia felt as if someone had punched her in the ribs. "You . . . . you knew about Kyra—that she was the one who leaked the media stories?"

He winced, apparently in some sudden, acute pain. Once he'd got himself back under control, he shook his head. "No, I believe that I knew it all along. My grandmother, she was never wrong about anything—about *anyone*—in her life." With his right hand, shaking noticeably, he reached up and indicated his temple. "She had something . . . a *gift* . . . to see the good in everyone. " He stared deeply into Alicia's eyes. "I know that you would never do anything like that to me. It's difficult. I have never been able to trust. But I can trust you." He paused another moment, then added, "I *love* you."

Alicia felt him squeeze her hand tightly.

Although she tried to hide her emotion—no doubt Gofreddo was struggling with his own recovery and could've done without any unnecessary drama—she couldn't stop a single tear from breaking free at the corner of her eye. It rolled down her cheek and clung to her chin.

Gofreddo reached out and wiped the tear away. "Things will be fine now," he said. "I can feel it."

Alicia remained there, at Gofreddo's side, for a while longer . . . it felt much longer than the five minutes which the doctor had prescribed. Not that Alicia had any complaints.

In the end, it was Gofreddo who spoke next.

He seemed somewhat panicked, and his reaction alarmed her.

Sitting up in bed, almost straightening his back, he said, "What about the Security team member—what about the one who *shot* me?"

Knowing that there was going to be no way to placate Gofreddo by simply telling him not to worry, Alicia reached up and pressed her finger to her earpiece.

She consulted with the Link.

With Mackenzie Angliss.

Once she'd got the reply, she turned back to Gofreddo, with an easy smile.

"She's fine," Alicia replied. "Relieved of duty for the next couple of days—but *fine*. She's been informed that you're okay." She smirked. "That she's not a murderer."

Gofreddo remained tense for several moments.

Alicia wondered if he was going to second guess her.

But, if he was considering whether or not she was telling the truth, he said nothing about it.

Perhaps that was what he meant by 'trusting' her . . . he had to force himself to *trust* her now; to *believe* whatever she told him was as honest as she could manage.

"May I ask you something?" Gofreddo said.

"What?"

"Can you give me a kiss?"

29

CULINARY CELEBRATION

licia raced about the Orbital Café kitchen.

A saucepan clattered at her feet.

She swore under her breath.

This time she managed to keep herself from *crying* out.

With a swift back heel, she slammed the oven door closed.

She'd got herself up early that morning—*earlier than usual*—so that she could come in before anyone else arrived. To be here, to be in the kitchen, it felt almost like being back home, on the family farm. She recalled how her grandmother would wake her up so that they might do some baking. As she rubbed the sleep from her eyes, there would always be those few moments when Alicia felt great resentment for her grandmother. But once they got down into the kitchen. Once they began to get their hands messy with the ingredients, it was almost like Alicia had entered another plane. Almost as if they'd entered another plane *together*.

By the time the rest of the family rose up out of their beds and came down to the kitchen for their breakfast, Alicia and her

244

grandmother would've prepared all manner of delicious treats: pancakes, an apple tart, muffins. It was always worth the unpleasant waking-up part for the looks on her family's faces.

This morning, Alicia was working hard at putting together a chocolate cake. She had gone just a little crazy with the chocolate filling; not to mention the frosting. To be honest, this wasn't really an opportunity to show off her talents. This was simple, straightforward, heartfelt cooking.

Straight from the soul.

She had wanted to thank her staff for their hard work during the lunar eclipse, and the best way she could think to do it was through the medium of a chocolate cake.

Now that the cake was in the oven, and cooking away, she allowed herself a moment of respite. A moment to take stock.

She always enjoyed these silent—*lonely*—moments, before the majority of the Celestial Stays Dome had risen out of their beds.

It was then that Alicia heard the footsteps outside.

A skitter ran up her spine.

How many times had the sound of footsteps outside the kitchen proven the precursor to some terrible happening; to some unexpected—*unwanted*—guest?

It was almost like some bad dream.

He was back again.

Back in *her* kitchen again.

Julius Denisov.

Although she knew she shouldn't do anything of the sort, she couldn't help but slip a glance to the knife rack. She checked over the sharp blades and knew, if she had to do it—if she *really* had to do it—then she could grab hold of one.

And fight her corner.

Julius attempted a smile but quickly aborted it.

He seemed to *trudge* toward her.

Alicia wondered what she'd ever seen in him.

Had she ever seen anything in him?

It calmed her nerves when Julius came to a halt still several paces away.

When she took in his face, the dark bags beneath his eyes, she realised that he must've come straight over from the Stellar Tide; that he was probably on his way home from the night shift.

"I was hoping to catch you," he said. "I know that you come in here early—that you're dedicated to your work. I wanted to have the chance to speak with you alone." He halted for a long second, as if he needed to work out how to phrase what he had to say perfectly. "I wanted to *apologise* personally for my behaviour."

Alicia felt a prickling sensation across the surface of her skin.

Her chest tightened.

Her blood ran cool.

"It was wrong for me to continue to pursue you, when you made it clear that things were over between us." He dipped his head, as if he was a cartoonist's impression of someone who was ashamed. "I hope that you'll be happy with Gofreddo." He glanced up now, met her eye. "From everything I hear, he's a stand-out guy"—he managed a smile—"I'm sure you'll be happy together."

Alicia remained completely still.

She was waiting for the punchline.

Would there be one coming?

Her pulse tapped along, as if anticipating a sting soon to arrive.

Julius *surely* hadn't simply come here to do what he'd said . . . had he?

But, without anything more to say, he turned away and headed for the doorway.

Alicia surprised even herself when she broke free of the spot and went after him, catching up before he had a chance to leave the kitchen. As she laid her hand on his shoulder, gently turning him back around, she thought about all the times she'd willed him *gone* from not just her kitchen but from the Moon too . . .

When their eyes met, there was no need for words.

Alicia simply wrapped her arms about him.

They embraced for a few seconds.

And then they parted.

With a gentle smile—almost a shadow of his former 'charming' grin—he said, "I'm proud of you, you know? Proud of how you've done. How you've managed to . . ." Here he trailed off, then scratched the back of his neck, apparently a touch embarrassed. "Well," he went on, finally, "I guess I shouldn't give it away . . ."

"Give *what* away?" Alicia said.

He jerked his thumb in the direction of the customer area of the Orbital Café. "Supervisor Habiba Nuha is waiting for you . . ."

Just when Alicia had felt her whole body cool—just when she'd managed to collect her thoughts back together and feel like things were going back to normal—she felt her gut stretching tight all over again.

She turned back to Julius, remembering herself, remembering what'd just passed between them—what'd passed between them in the none-too-distant past.

"Thank you," she said, looking into his eyes. "Thanks for making things right."

Julius blushed slightly, but he made no reply.

He only inclined his head and then found his way out.

Although Julius hadn't exactly *lied* about who awaited Alicia in the customer area of the Orbital Café, he had certainly 'omitted certain truths'.

Because it wasn't just Supervisor Habiba waiting there.

Mackenzie Angliss was there also.

As Alicia emerged from the kitchen, she breathed in the steady, sweet scent of the chocolate cake baking in the oven. She was beginning to feel anxious about her preparations; about whether or not the cake would be ready by the time her kitchen staff turned up for work. All the same, it wasn't like she could blow off *two* of her bosses . . . so she sat down at the table with them.

"Alicia," Mackenzie said, beginning the conversation. "I just wanted to say sorry for everything; for having misinterpreted the situation . . . for choosing to believe *gossip* rather than hard and fast evidence."

Alicia just felt *awkward* more than anything.

Even though she'd done nothing to find herself being falsely accused of leaking information to the media about Gofreddo Zito . . . well, aside from allowing herself to get close to him.

Really *quite* close.

"That done with," Mackenzie said, frictionlessly moving onto the next matter, "it's probably worthwhile you knowing at this point that Supervisor Habiba here is planning on leaving at the end of her rotation."

Of course from the frank personal conversations she'd had with Habiba, Alicia had suspected this had been coming. But that didn't mean it was any less impactful to actually hear the decision being spoken out loud. She glanced to Habiba, and Habiba smiled back at her.

"Now," Mackenzie said, continuing, "this of course presents the issue of who will replace her—who will take up the mantel of

Supervisor of Catering." She paused for a moment, sniffing at the air. "Gee, something smells good."

"I'm doing some baking," Alicia replied, absentmindedly. "It won't be ready for half an hour yet."

Mackenzie grimaced. "Probably for the best—I don't think my figure would much appreciate me indulging in something chocolatey and sweet . . ." Finally, Mackenzie caught the nub of what she'd been saying. "So, Alicia, the question we've come here this morning to ask is whether or not you'd be willing to take on the role."

Alicia allowed the words to trickle through her for several seconds.

She still couldn't quite stretch her mind into believing it.

And yet Mackenzie couldn't have spoken any more plainly.

Worried that she might not be able to form the words, Alicia surprised herself that she had the strength to utter, "Of *course!*"

"Good," Mackenzie said with a smile.

She glanced to Habiba, who Alicia could see had a veneer of tears in her eyes.

It would be difficult to give up all the work she'd put in, Alicia could see that, but she would be certain to make Habiba proud . . . to show that the great progress she'd made hadn't been in vain; that it would be her *legacy*.

Mackenzie sniffed at the air again.

Frowned.

"Can I smell . . . *burning?*" she said.

Alicia leaped out of her seat.

3 0

EXIT CLEARANCE

*O*nce *Alicia had served* the chocolate cake to all of her
kitchen staff, she felt somewhat deflated, as she always
tended to feel after she'd woken up early. There had been lots of
grinning faces; clearly lots of satisfied *stomachs*. It gave Alicia a
gentle, warming feeling which clamoured in the centre of her
chest, and through her blood.

Because there were very few guests present at the Orbital Café,
and because Mackenzie had given Alicia permission to close up
shop for a few days of—what Mackenzie termed—'well-deserved'
leave, Alicia allowed her staff to go free once they'd finished with
their respective slices of chocolate cake.

As she took care of the security protocols involved with 'shut-
ting up shop', Alicia couldn't help but notice the PEAR which
settled down on the Orbital Café landing pad.

For some reason, she suspected that it might be Gofreddo, that
he might be coming by to pick her up and carry her off on another

lunar escapade . . . not that Alicia had the slightest inkling of refusing such a proposal.

However, it wasn't Gofreddo.

As the PEAR settled down on the landing pad, Alicia soon saw the familiar figure of Wendy Flowme emerge from within. Her silver hair lent her a noble air. As she stepped closer, Alicia couldn't help but think of the last time they'd met . . . when Wendy had told her—in no uncertain terms—that she was to leave Gofreddo alone.

Once Wendy stood a few paces away, she halted, then said, "Before we go any further, I want to apologise about the other day —about those . . . *things* I said to you . . . none of them were deserved." She paused in thought for a moment. "You have to understand that, in these past few months, I've grown very close to the Zito family—they have become, not to put too metaphorical a point on it, *dear* to me . . . that said, it's one thing to be protective, and another to slander someone without evidence." She paused again, then added, "I'm sorry."

Alicia couldn't help but smile by way of reply. "I wouldn't worry too much about it," she said. "Did you come all the way over to the café just to say that?"

Wendy grinned. "Actually, I came over to congratulate you on your new appointment—*Supervisor*, that's something I certainly have no experience of. I'm sure you'll do a grand job of it, though . . ."

"What about you?" Alicia said. "Don't you have any plans to come back—to return to the Crescent Gardens?"

Wendy shook her head. "I think I'll be just fine Earthside for the time being—I think there's enough for me to sink my teeth into."

"You dirty *beast*, you," Alicia replied, smiling wider still.

"Nah," Wendy said, "I'm planning on shoving off—leaving this hunk of rock and dust behind for good." She glanced around her, almost with a nostalgic air. "Can't say I'll miss it *terribly*." She looked up, to the Earth as it hung above them. "Although perhaps I'll miss *some* things."

The two of them lost themselves in the giant, swirling, blue orb above them.

In the end, Wendy was the one to cut through the silence.

"So," she said, reaching out to take hold of Alicia's arm by the crook of the elbow. "Feel like escorting an old chancer onto her plane?"

On their way to the terminal in the PEAR, Wendy explained to Alicia about how Gofreddo had made a point of ensuring that Lan Niu was okay; that she hadn't been traumatised by her shooting him. Wendy revealed that she'd gone along with Gofreddo to personally meet with Lan Niu and assure her that she hadn't been at fault. Although the girl had clearly been shaken up, she'd seemed to at least see some sense. The hope was that she'd return to duty in the next few days.

What surprised Alicia all the more, though, was that Gofreddo had pulled all sorts of strings so that Kyra might be able to remain on the Moon. There was, of course, the matter of the many Celestial Stays rules and regulations she had bent—and outright *broken* —but Gofreddo had been clear that he hadn't any interest in seeing her punished . . .

Alicia couldn't say whether she might be as forgiving.

Just *how* Kyra could remain on the Moon in good conscience after what she'd done, Alicia couldn't quite understand.

Wendy informed Alicia of how Kyra had also placed a camera in the dress she had used for the funeral. That was how the media on Earth had got hold of the pictures. It made Alicia shudder to think about how she'd been used.

So many people had apologised to her in the past few days.

Would there be room for one more?

And would Alicia even be able to forgive Kyra?

After all, what she'd done was oddly similar to that which Gofreddo had *believed* she had done to him. Kyra had earned Alicia's trust through deceit, and then she had taken advantage of that trust.

In fact, if anyone owed her an apology, it was Kyra.

In some ways, Alicia believed that she had been just as wronged by Kyra as Gofreddo had been.

But, then again, perhaps if Gofreddo had managed to forgive her then she could do the same . . . only time would tell.

Hopefully Kyra would simply cut her losses and leave the Moon.

Leave all this behind.

Leave her *deception* behind . . .

As the PEAR circled on the terminal landing pad, Alicia took in the familiar figure of Gofreddo standing there. She noted another pair of figures standing by, too.

When the PEAR had come in closer to the lunar surface, she realised that it was Louise and Njhay . . . that they, of course, had come to see Wendy off on her trip back to Earth.

Alicia gave Wendy a final hug and then handed her over to Louise, so that the two of them might speak frankly before Wendy took her leave of the Moon.

On her way away from the group, and into Gofreddo's private company, Louise managed to get in a quick word. "Congratulations," Louise said. "*Supervisor*, well, I guess I'm going to have to watch my step around you."

"Damn right," Alicia said, remaining firm-faced for precisely two seconds before breaking out into an uncontrollable grin.

Alicia left Louise and Wendy behind.

She turned all her attention onto Gofreddo.

Onto his searing blue eyes.

"Aren't you going to say goodbye to Wendy?" Alicia said.

Gofreddo gave a shrug. "We already did that part back in the Lunar Grand where she was staying with my grandmother." He glanced over to Louise and Wendy, and Alicia saw the two of them weeping freely now as Njhay watched on in that useless —*male*—way.

Gofreddo turned back to Alicia.

"I think I'm done with goodbyes for a while."

With that comment, he reached his arm around Alicia's shoulders, shepherding her away from the departure scene.

Once they were alone—*truly alone*—outside the terminal, Alicia allowed herself to turn fully into Gofreddo. She felt his gentle body warmth. She breathed in his unmistakable, musky scent. And, just because she could, she reached out and laid her palm flat against his rippling stomach muscles.

"You know what's going to happen next, don't you?" Gofreddo said.

Alicia felt her whole body tremble.

Of course, superficially, she knew what was going to happen next . . . at least in the medium term . . .

"What've you got in mind?" she said.

Gofreddo smiled slightly.

In the distance, Alicia could hear the rumble of thrusters starting up.

Of the tin can which'd carry Wendy back to Earth coming to life.

She breathed more of Gofreddo in.

He *intoxicated* her.

"Well," Gofreddo said, "I think it's time for me to get serious." He glanced down at her. "You decided to get serious, after all." He smirked. "A Supervisor . . . I should take care."

Alicia shifted herself away from Gofreddo.

She held a mock blaming finger to him, wagging it just a short distance from the tip of his nose. "You know," she said. "You're the *second* person who's made that joke in the past hour."

"Who says it was a joke?" Gofreddo replied, still smiling to himself.

Alicia narrowed her eyes.

Then realised she couldn't stay angry with him.

It was *impossible* to stay angry with someone so hot.

"So," she said, "what've you got in mind?"

The rumble of the thrusters became louder still.

Alicia could feel the vibrations passing through the ground under her feet.

It shook her down to the bones.

A rocket returning to Earth.

And *she* wasn't on it.

At one point, she'd been certain that she *would* be . . .

As the rocket rose up above the terminal, taking to space, leaving the Moon behind, they stood dazzled by its trajectory. Alicia wondered if either one of them would say anything ever again.

Then Gofreddo continued his thoughts from where he'd left off.

"I'd like to make my grandfather proud," he said. "And it's time that I put together something to *really* do his name justice."

He hesitated.

Alicia could tell that he was still having trouble placing his trust in her—placing his trust in *anyone* . . . how did he *know* that she wouldn't betray him?

Feeling his emotions seeping from his pores, she reached down and gave his hand a squeeze.

"I want to explore. " He turned his attention to Alicia. "And I want to take you with me . . . what would you say?"

Alicia felt herself stunned by the request for several seconds.

She took a deep breath.

"Well," she said, "that depends what you mean . . . 'explore' *how?*"

"Outer space," Gofreddo replied. "That is what would make my grandfather proudest, I am sure; and it is what would be the best use of my father's resources." A smile tweaked the corners of his mouth. "That *inheritance* he seems so intent on giving me."

Alicia felt a few doubts creeping in, but she shoved them away.

It was *fine* to doubt . . . it was fine to be afraid.

"And when do you plan on putting this into place?" she said.

"After our rotation finishes," he replied, squeezing Alicia tighter. "We will need a Ship's Cook, that much is for sure, and I hear you have some really *excellent* references."

Alicia allowed the warmth to fill her up.

Her whole body felt as if it might catch fire.

She reached down, took hold of Gofreddo's hand, holding it tighter still.

"Come on, Romeo," she said. "Let's go and have ourselves some good vacations. Then we'll talk."

As Alicia led them to the PEAR which'd just descended on the landing pad outside the terminal, she realised that she had a skip in her step.

More than that, though.

She realised she was grinning from ear to ear.

Whatever happened—whatever happened *next*—she knew that whenever Gofreddo was nearby she would never be far from adventure.

And wasn't that what she'd always craved?

THE END

AUTHOR'S NOTE

Thank you for taking the time to read one of my books. If you would like to hear about my latest releases you can sign up for my newsletter here: www.essiepowers.com

Thanks for reading!

Essie Powers

Orbital Eclipse
The Second Lunar Lovescape Novel

Copyright © Essie Powers, 2016.
Published by DIB Books
All rights reserved.

Cover design and layout copyright © DIB Books, 2016.
Cover art copyright © Sergey Nivens / Shutterstock, 2015.

This work is fictional. None of the characters or events depicted in this book are based on real life and any resemblance to real events or persons is purely coincidental.

Neither this book, nor any part of it, may be reproduced without express permission from the publisher.

www.ingramcontent.com/pod-product-compliance
Lightning Source LLC
Chambersburg PA
CBHW031211260626
47169CB00007B/2020